My name is Barry Allen, and I am the fastest man alive. A freak accident sent a lightning bolt into my lab one night, dousing me with electricity and chemicals, gifting me with superspeed. Since then, I've used my powers to fight the good fight, protecting my city, my world, and my universe from all manner of threats. I've stared down crazed speedsters, time-traveling techno-magicians, and every sort of thief, crook, and lunatic you can imagine.

    With the help of my friends and my adopted family, I run S.T.A.R. Labs, a hub of super-science, and use it as a staging base to keep Central City safe from those who would cause it harm.

    I've traveled to not one but two different futures, and I've seen the amazing heights to which humanity will soar. In the present, I do everything I can to help get us there.

    I am . . .

THE FLASH

BY BARRY LYGA

SH™

CROSSOVER CRISIS

SUPERGIRL'S SACRIFICE

AMULET BOOKS
NEW YORK

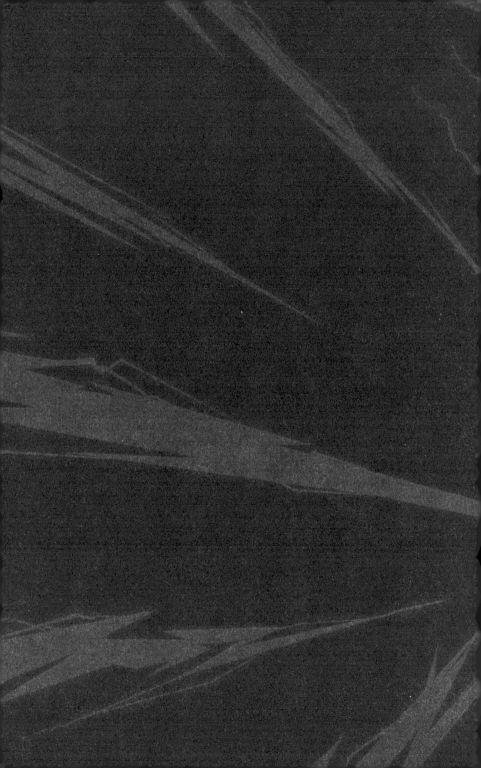

Library of Congress Control Number 2020931620

ISBN 978-1-4197-3739-8

Cover Illustration by Shawn M Moll
Book design by Brenda E. Angelilli

Supergirl is based on characters created by Jerry Siegel and Joe Schuster.
By special arrangement with the Jerry Siegel family.

Printed and bound in U.S.A.
10 9 8 7 6 5 4 3 2 1

Amulet Books are available at special discounts when purchased in quantity for premiums and promotions as well as fundraising or educational use. Special editions can also be created to specification. For details, contact specialsales @abramsbooks.com or the address below.

Amulet Books® is a registered trademark of Harry N. Abrams, Inc.

ABRAMS The Art of Books
195 Broadway, New York, NY 10007
abramsbooks.com

PREVIOUSLY IN

Disaster has struck on multiple fronts! In Central City, the Flash and Green Arrow only barely were able to stop the nearly omnipotent living weapon known as Anti-Matter Man from coming through a rip in reality to destroy Earth 1. They were too late to save Earth 27, unfortunately, and now Central City is host to ten thousand displaced superspeed refugees from a parallel universe.

Meanwhile, in Star City, a serial bomber destroyed several buildings as part of a plot to steal teleportation technology and high-tech robot bees. Now the city—and Detective Joe West and Team Arrow—must contend with the madcap lunacy of . . . Ambush Bug! Plus, Cisco and Mr. Terrific have been blown out of this world and lost somewhere in time.

Speaking of time . . . The Legends of Tomorrow have had their ship destroyed by a force no one understands. And meanwhile, Owlman—the evil Bruce Wayne from Earth 27—is lurking on Earth 1, preparing to do who knows what . . .

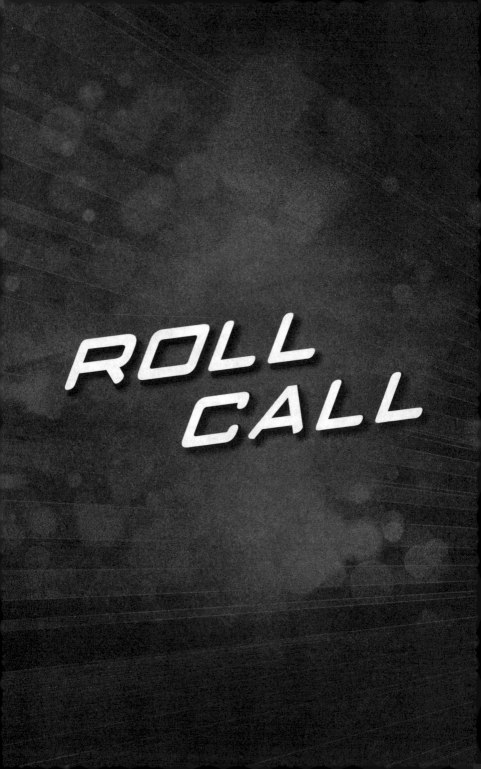

EARTH 1

THE FLASH (BARRY ALLEN)
IRIS WEST-ALLEN
GREEN ARROW (OLIVER QUEEN)
DR. CAITLIN SNOW
OVERWATCH (FELICITY SMOAK)
DETECTIVE JOE WEST
VIBE (CISCO RAMON)
BLACK CANARY (DINAH DRAKE)
SPARTAN (JOHN DIGGLE)
MR. TERRIFIC (CURTIS HOLT)

EARTH 38

SUPERGIRL
(KARA ZOR-EL/KARA DANVERS)
SUPERMAN (KAL-EL/CLARK KENT)
MARTIAN MANHUNTER
(J'ONN J'ONZZ)
BRAINIAC 5 (QUERL DOX)
DEO DIRECTOR ALEX DANVERS
GUARDIAN (JAMES OLSEN)

THE LEGENDS
OF TOMORROW

HEAT WAVE (MICK RORY)
AVA SHARPE

AND

OWLMAN (BRUCE WAYNE)

N THE PRIVACY OF HER OFFICE, AVA Sharpe squeezed her eyes shut tight and groaned deep in her throat. She was the director of the Time Bureau, a beyond–top secret government organization devoted to policing the time stream and keeping history on track. The pressures that came with that job were almost unimaginable, and usually she dealt with them through a combination of rigid authority and no-nonsense organization.

Sometimes, though, like right now, it felt as though she'd been caught in a rainstorm with nothing but an old newspaper for an umbrella.

A part of her wondered if non-clones ever felt so completely overwhelmed. She had been designed and programmed by the original Time Master, Rip Hunter, to be the pinnacle of human perfection, but on days like this, she wondered if maybe Rip had dropped a codon here or there in his genetic manipulation, if the folks who'd grown her at Advanced Variant Automation

Corporation had goofed up and made her slightly more suscep-
tible to deep, deep frustration.

No, she figured. Everyone felt this way sometimes. In fact,
she reasoned, her annoyance was one of the things that proved
she was human, albeit in convenient duplicate form. And if she
was the height of human development, then maybe her frustration was the apex of all human frustration, too.

Sure, that made sense.

"Is it the tuna?" a voice asked.

Ava looked up. She'd thought she was alone in her office, but
at some point, as she'd been staring fruitlessly at the insides of her
eyelids, Gary Green had sneaked in. Gary was long and lanky,
his limbs dangling, as though they knew they didn't belong and
would run off on their own at the first sign of danger.

She trusted Gary. She wasn't quite sure *why*, but she
did. What he lacked in competence, he made up for in loyalty
and verve.

"Is *what* the tuna?" Ava demanded.

Gary swallowed hard, adjusted his glasses, and pointed
wordlessly to her desk. A half-eaten tuna on rye rested amid
the crumb remains of a bag of potato chips. "I lied," he told
her. "That sandwich was in the fridge for two days, not one. I
thought it would be OK, but . . ."

Ava grunted and swept the detritus of her lunch into the
trash can next to her desk. "It's not the sandwich, Gary. It's the
situation. Things are out of hand." *The time is out of joint*, she
thought suddenly. Shakespeare. *Hamlet*. She grimaced. Most
people would remember that from high school, or maybe an

English course in college. Not Ava. She remembered it because it had been implanted in her brain, along with false memories of a childhood she'd never had.

The only memories she trusted for real were the ones she knew she'd made herself since rolling off the clone "assembly line" and working at the Time Bureau. Those were the only ones that mattered. Her work. Her friends.

Sara . . .

Sara, who was missing . . .

"Well, uh, Iris West-Allen called," Gary said, wagging a slip of paper in the air. "Again."

"That's the third time today so far," Ava told him.

"And five yesterday," he said, nodding. "And four the day before that."

Iris had been calling with increasing urgency for a couple of days now, ever since some kind of hole in reality had opened up in Central City. From what Ava could tell, the Flash had handled that problem. She had bigger issues to deal with. She literally had no time for Iris West-Allen and Central City.

The time is out of joint . . .

"What did she say this time?" Ava didn't really want to ask, but she knew Gary wouldn't leave her alone until he'd delivered Iris's message.

Gary cleared his throat and consulted the paper. "'Tell Ms. Sharpe that if a human being can move fast enough, it's possible to vibrate one's molecules to the point that one can phase through solid matter.'" Gary frowned. "That can't actually be true, can it?"

"It is," said the Flash as he vibrated through the wall behind Ava's desk. "Flash Fact!"

Ava jumped out of her seat. Gary shrieked in a warbling falsetto and slapped at his waist, searching for a weapon that wasn't there.

"It's a ghost!" Gary screamed. "It's a ghost!"

"It's not a ghost!" Ava snapped. Her heart raced as she leaned against her desk for support. "You can't just do that to people!" she told the Flash.

He grinned under his cowl. "Well, you weren't returning our calls. I was in the neighborhood, so I thought I'd stop by in person."

Gary turned to run from the room, forgot to open the door, and banged into it full force. "Oh!" he cried.

Ava sighed heavily. "Gary, go put some ice on your face. And don't tell anyone about our guest here."

Pinching his nose to stanch the bleeding, Gary nodded somewhat morosely and slouched out of the office, closing the door behind him.

"I'm very busy," Ava told the Flash. "Make it quick."

Another grin. "Quick is what I do best. We've got some time travel troubles. Two of our teammates have been missing for a couple of days now, and we need to get them out of the time stream, wherever they are." He paused. "Well, *when*ever, I guess."

Ava shook her head as the Flash explained further: While closing the breach in Central City—"Which saved the whole world from dying a horrible death, you're welcome"—three people had been shunted into the time stream. Green Arrow had been tossed into the near future and safely popped up a couple of hours later. But Cisco Ramon and Mr. Terrific were still missing.

"We don't know if they're in the past or the future," the Flash told her. "But we figure the Legends can do a sweep through the time stream looking for Cisco's unique vibrational—"

"I'm gonna stop you there, Twinkletoes." Ava held up a hand to shut him up. "I can't have the Legends help you because I don't know where they are. Or when," she added quickly. Stupid time travel.

"What do you mean?"

With a growl of annoyance, Ava snatched up a sheaf of papers from her desk. "These are temporal incident reports," she said. "Something happened to the *Waverider* a couple of days ago. The team was in the temporal zone, researching this 'Flashpoint' aberration you told them about. And then we just stopped hearing from them."

The Flash's lips pressed into a grim, set line. "No distress call?"

"Nothing. They just . . ." She popped open the fingers on one hand in a *poof! gone!* gesture. "It's been days, and we've heard nothing at all. No telemetry from Gideon. No temporal beacon. Nothing."

"A couple of days ago . . ." the Flash mused. "That's when the hole in reality opened up and Anti-Matter Man threatened to come through. Do you think the two are related?"

"How would I know?" Ava threw down the papers. "All I

know is, my top team is missing. *Gone*. Including, by the way, the woman I love. And we have no way of finding them."

"You have other methods of time travel, don't you?" he asked.

She raised her arm so that her sleeve fell back, revealing the super-high-tech bracelet she wore on her wrist. It was called a Time Courier, and it was designed to let her travel through time and space with ease. The technology was expensive and dangerous, so only specific, highly trusted members of the Time Bureau possessed and used them. As director, Ava always wore one, and it could take her anywhere at any time. But in this case . . .

"We don't know where to start looking, Flash. Same reason you just can't go running through time to look for *your* friends. It's a big time stream out there. And a big Multiverse, too. Forget looking for a needle in a haystack . . ."

"This is like looking for the tip of a needle in all the hay in the world," the Flash finished.

"Something like that," she said.

He pursed his lips and pondered. "OK," he said, and she wondered how much superfast thinking he'd done in those couple of seconds. Yes, she was the peak of human development, but the Flash was beyond human. "There are some things we can still try. I'll stay in touch."

He started to vibrate through the wall, then stopped. "And Ms. Sharpe? From now on, please answer when we call. It'll make things go easier."

She nodded mutely and watched him phase through her

office wall, running off to do . . . whatever it was super-people did when they needed to save the world.

The world, she feared, desperately needed saving.

The time is out of joint, she thought again, then finished the quotation out loud:

"O cursèd spite, / That ever I was born to set it right!"

REIGN OF ERROR!

TELEPORTING MADMAN BAFFLES COPS, CITIZENS FOR TWO DAYS

For two days now, Star City has been under attack. This may seem like old hat to most denizens of the city, but this attack is different from the usual fare we've dealt with over the years. There is no man-made earthquake, no outlandish clan of ninjas running pell-mell through downtown at night. There are no firefights on the streets or explosions.

What there is, however, is Ambush Bug.

This green-clad, antennae-bearing chaos agent has spent the past two days turning Star City into his own personal gallery of japes, practical jokes, and madcap lunacy. No one is safe, from the kids playing baseball in Kirby Park (who were subject to a lengthy rundown as Ambush Bug teleported from home plate to third and back again, throwing the ball to and from himself) to the mayor's office, where aides confirm that the mayor's custom bulletproof limousine was, in fact, stalled out when a large pear was inserted into the tailpipe.

Your intrepid columnist reached out to some of your fellow Star Citizens to get their opinion on this "Ambush Bug." In fact, I was able to get ahold of Rene Ramirez. You may remember him as Mayor Oliver Queen's aide during Queen's tenure running the city.

"This isn't like Central City, where crazy things happen all the time," complained Ramirez. "This is Star City. This is a serious town!"

As soon as he finished speaking, Mr. Ramirez was hit with multiple water balloons that seemed to appear from nowhere.

Others were not quite so saturnine.

"Is it even illegal, what he's doing?" said a citizen who preferred to remain anonymous. "Playing pranks on people? You ask me, this town could use some lightening up."

At that moment, Ambush Bug appeared from thin air and dumped a quart of diet soda on your columnist's head, chortling, "Get it? Lighten up? You could definitely stand to switch to diet, Jackie Boy!"

(I report this next fact purely in the interests of full disclosure: My weight is currently 183 pounds, well within the acceptable range for a man of my height.)

However amusing one may or may not find his pranks, Ambush Bug's "reign of error" has had serious consequences for Star City. Concerned citizens have taken to patrolling the streets in loosely aligned vigilante gangs, with violence breaking out on many occasions. Local hospital emergency rooms are at capacity with not only victims of the Bug's pranks but also those who've been injured in the cross fire when citizen posses have attempted to capture Ambush Bug on their own.

Given Oliver Queen's experience with matters that transcend the normal and the everyday, your intrepid columnist reached out to the former mayor for his thoughts, but all attempts were left unanswered. No one knows exactly where Oliver Queen is, in fact.

1

WITH THE WEATHER IN NATIONAL
City finally turning from a grim winter to a
pleasant and long-overdue spring, the tables
outside Noonan's were definitely in demand. But when Kara
Danvers arrived for brunch—late, of course—she was pleased to
see that her friends had already gotten a table. Good positioning,
too—far enough from the restaurant entrance that they wouldn't
be bothered by customers coming and going, but still far enough
from the street that the road noise wouldn't bother them, either.

"There she is!" James Olsen cried, and leaped to his feet,
applauding.

Before Kara could demur, the others followed suit—Lena
Luthor, Hank Henshaw, and of course her sister, Alex. They
all stood and clapped wildly. James even managed a piercing
whistle.

Kryptonians can blush just like anyone else, and Kara's
cheeks flamed red and hot with mingled embarrassment and

pride. All around her, patrons at other tables were joining in, even though they didn't really know why. There was just something infectious about applause, she supposed.

She essayed a brief little curtsy, which only spurred her friends on to even more applause.

"That's enough, you guys. Come on!" She waved them into silence and pulled over a chair. "Sheesh. Talk about embarrassing!"

"The youngest winner of the Wheeler-Nicholson Award in history!" Alex said. "That's something to cheer about."

"I was going to bring a big banner," James told her, gesturing as wide as his arms allowed. Given his height and arm span, that would make for a pretty darn huge banner. "About yea big. Lena voted it down."

"I knew you'd be thrown by even some clapping." Lena, Kara's best friend, leaned over and patted her hand. "I did my best to keep them all under control."

"Thanks. I appreciate it."

The Wheeler-Nicholson. After the Pulitzer, it was the most prestigious award in all of journalism, and now her name was added to the roster of those who'd achieved it. Maybe she *should* let her friends make a big deal. Just this once.

Kara looked around the table. Alex. James. Hank. (Or John. Or, more accurately, J'Onn, the Martian Manhunter.) Lena.

"Aren't we missing someone?" she asked.

Just then, a slender man with a thick mop of black hair sidled up to the table, hands clasped behind his back. Querl Dox, better known as Brainiac 5 or just Brainy, was a member of the Legion of Super-Heroes, a superpowered team from the thirty-first century. He had volunteered to spend some time in the primitive twenty-first century while Kara's friend Winn visited the future to help out the Legion. It was sort of like a temporal student exchange program, really.

"I apologize for my tardiness," he said. "I was unavoidably . . . delayed."

"He's addicted to Tetris," Alex said confidentially.

"You promised never to tell!" Brainy snapped. "My weakness is my own onus to bear, not a burden to be borne by those I call *friends*."

"It might be time for an intervention," said Hank.

"Says the man addicted to Chocos," Alex teased.

"I can quit anytime," Hank said. "I think."

"It's a fun game," Kara admitted. "There's no harm in getting caught up in it."

"I am on level seven thousand three hundred and twelve," Brainy confessed. "On that level, the . . . speed with which the pieces fall is quite exhilarating. And I find the music . . . jaunty."

"Oh, Brainy." Kara sighed. "You *do* have a problem, don't you?"

"Nothing that cannot be resolved with the application of huevos rancheros," Brainy said, sitting next to Kara. "Shall we order?"

James flagged down a waiter, and soon they were all ordering. Kara took another moment to look around the table as her friends laughed and chatted and caught up with one another. These moments—these messy, glorious moments of camaraderie—were what she lived for. No battle to wage. No super villains to thwart. Just sociability and friendship and love.

She'd lost a family when Krypton exploded. She'd found a new family on Earth when the Danverses adopted her. Then she'd rediscovered family on Argo, a surviving colony of Kryptonians that included her biological mother.

But this . . . This agglomeration around the table, this messy, chaotic, laughing, goofing collection that included the sister of a super villain, her cousin's best friend, a superhero from the future, a manhunter from Mars, and her own adoptive sister—this was the family she had built for herself. A family that had accreted around her. It was the family she was the most grateful for, one that came together through sheer force of will and mutual compassion. She loved them all so much.

"Look!" someone shouted at a nearby table.

"Up in the sky!" cried out someone else.

Kara did what everyone else did—she turned her attention skyward.

Unlike everyone else at the table, though, she could see quite a bit farther and much more clearly than mere mortals.

"Not a bird or a plane, I'd wager," J'Onn murmured.

With a combination of her telescopic vision and X-ray vision, Kara zoomed in on the thing overhead and tried to pierce the veil of smoke and flame surrounding it. It was roughly human-sized, she could tell, moving at an incredible speed in an arc over the city. Something—someone?—had hurled it with tremendous force across the sky, originating from who knew where. There was something in the composition of all that smoke that made it impossible for her to penetrate even with her X-ray vision, but she could tell that the thing's flight path was rapidly descending and that it would crash-land . . .

"In Governor's Park," she whispered.

At this time of day, with such gorgeous weather, the park would be teeming with families. It was one of National City's most popular spots on a beautiful day like today.

"I'm on it," J'Onn said with a brief glance at Kara. "Don't worry, anyone."

Kara clenched her fists. She was out in public. And even though Alex, James, and Brainy knew her true identity, Lena didn't, so she was stuck. J'Onn could run off because Lena knew he was the Martian Manhunter. But there was no ready excuse for Kara to—

James broke into her thoughts. "Kara, get to the CatCo offices and coordinate our team response to this!" He dropped a wink that Lena didn't see.

Kara breathed a sigh of relief and leaped up from her chair. "Will do, boss!" She favored him with a grateful smile and dashed away from the table with nary a farewell to any of the others.

An instant later, she ducked behind a stand of trees planted at the edge of the road to shield Noonan's from some of the street noise. No one could see her. At superspeed, she whipped off her Kara Danvers clothing, revealing the costume of Supergirl beneath. Half a second later, she was airborne, closing in on the hurtling object.

Supergirl, are you nearby?

The voice in her head was the Martian Manhunter. Telepathic communication always felt like remembering something mundane and long forgotten. She never got used to it.

I'm close by, J'Onn.

I'm going to start clearing the park, he told her. *But there are a lot of people. I need your help.*

Before she could respond, Kara "heard" a new voice intrude on the telepathic conversation. *Forgive me for hacking into your metaneural discussion*, said Brainiac 5, *but I wanted to tell you that Guardian and I are both en route to the park, as is Alex. And a DEO team has been scrambled, much like the eggs in my huevos rancheros.*

The DEO—the Department of Extra-Normal Operations— was a top secret government agency charged with protecting Earth from aliens and all sorts of superhuman threats. Alex was its director, and she was quite simply the best at her job. But at the end of the day, the DEO was still made up of human beings and they had the limitations of human beings. A team of agents wouldn't get to the park before the object crashed down, possibly killing hundreds of innocent people.

Supergirl considered for a split second. Her original plan had been to grab the object out of the sky. But it was moving with such incredible velocity that she couldn't be sure she would be able to stop it. There was a very good chance that its momentum would carry both it and her into the park, doubling the damage.

It was faster to take a straight shot to the park and help

J'Onn clear the area. She adjusted her flight path in midair and launched herself downward, fists out.

I've calculated the most likely collision point, Brainy told her and J'Onn, *based on current trajectory, prevailing wind patterns, and local gravity permutations. Impact is ninety-nine point two seven percent likely to occur within six meters of the carousel.*

The carousel. Great. If there was one place in the park guaranteed to be packed with kids and their parents at this time of day, it was the park's famous merry-go-round, which boasted three tiers of wooden horses, unicorns, winged frogs, and seahorses for kids to ride. In her mind's eye, Supergirl could see the moment of impact . . . the explosion of force as the carousel was smashed to pieces . . . bodies tossed into the air . . .

Nope. Not on my watch.

Well said! Brainy cheered.

Supergirl accelerated, then rapidly decelerated as the carousel hove into view. The Martian Manhunter was already there, snatching up a pair of kids and hustling them away. Supergirl landed just to the left of the merry-go-round and shouted, "Attention! Attention! We need to evacuate you! Now! Don't worry—everything will be all right!"

Then she moved at superspeed, grabbing up kids and their parents and shuttling them away to the edge of the park, where emergency services—alerted by the DEO, no doubt—were already stationed. She made ten trips in less than a minute, slowing down only to make certain she didn't hurt anyone while whisking them to safety. On her return to the carousel, she spied Brainy, Guardian, and Alex all hustling kids away from the impact zone.

Before she could say anything to her sister, her super-hearing picked up a whistling sound. She looked up again. The object had just breached the park's tree line and was now on its downward trajectory.

Ninety-nine point five nine percent chance now, Brainy told her.

"We don't need the updates!" she yelled, forgetting that she could speak to him with her mind. "Just keep moving people out of the way."

Brainy very calmly plucked a screaming toddler off the ground and levitated away, thanks to his Legion flight ring. *You don't have to scream,* he said. *I once evacuated the entire planet Mordan in time to save the inhabitants from the Fatal Five and a sun going nova.*

Sorry, she thought back to him. Then: *J'Onn? How are we doing?* She was keeping an eye on the object as it sped toward her.

All civilians evacuated within a one-hundred-meter radius. Get out of there, Supergirl!

She considered doing it. But who knew what would happen when this thing hit the ground? She wanted to be close by to contain an explosion or subdue a creature or whatever needed to be done.

Nah, she thought to him. *I'm going to stay and watch the fireworks.*

Supergirl! J'Onn screamed. Her head pulsed for a moment with something like a migraine. *Don't be stupid! Drop back!*

The object was practically on top of her now. It crackled and spat green-and-blue flames as it shrieked through the air at her. Her X-ray vision caught a break as some of the smoke parted and she thought she saw . . .

She dodged to one side as the thing hurtled past her. The air went hot and dry in its wake, choked with clouds of smoke, ash, and soot. With a thunderous roar, it hit the ground just in front of the carousel. The earth shook—she flashed back to the last moments of Krypton, as groundquakes wracked the planet, ferocious power trembling up from the radioactive, unstable core. Her parents put her in a rocket and launched her into space . . .

But this wasn't Krypton. It was Earth, and the planet wasn't exploding. Before her, the world had gone black and gray with smoke and dirt thrown into the air. She heard flames and the sizzle-crack of melting metal. There would be no rides on the carousel for quite a while.

Supergirl drew in a deep breath, then exhaled her superbreath, blowing a tunnel through the debris hanging in the air. A deep furrow had been carved into the ground in front of her, leading ahead toward what had once been the carousel. The metal framework looked like a birthday cake that had been left out in the sun too long, and the wooden animals were all singed and flickering with flames. She shuddered in horror but also in relief that they'd managed to evacuate the area.

Supergirl! J'Onn called. *Supergirl! Are you OK?*

Yep. She took a step forward and blew some more ash out of the way, then squinted at the clouds of particulate all around her. *Let's get a hazmat team in here. My microscopic vision isn't picking up anything alien or dangerous in the debris field, but we can't be too sure.*

I'll tell Alex. You're sure you're OK?

She grinned to herself. As Hank Henshaw, J'Onn affected the stern mien of a driving taskmaster, but the truth was that he saw in Supergirl and Alex reflections of his own departed Martian daughters. His fatherly affection was sweet, even when unnecessary.

Takes a lot to hurt me. Hang back and help emergency services. I'm going to check on this thing.

She walked along the gash the fallen object had cut into the ground. The furrow deepened as it progressed. A few feet from the carousel, it stopped, ending in a slightly wider crater.

Supergirl peered down there.

And gasped.

Lying in a four-foot-deep pit, smoke purling from his body, was none other than Superman.

And he wasn't moving.

2

BARRY ALLEN—THE FLASH—GRIMACED as he listened to the report from Star City. He stood in the center of the Cortex, the huge, circular chamber at the heart of S.T.A.R. Labs that served as a staging area for Team Flash. On the main monitor, Joe West was filling him in on the hunt for Ambush Bug. A hunt that was, by every metric that mattered, not going well.

". . . not that I'm making excuses or anything," Joe was saying, "but chasing a teleporter isn't easy."

"I've been there," Barry said, remembering chasing Shawna Baez, the teleporting metahuman criminal also known as Peekaboo. He'd finally captured her by shutting down the lights in a tunnel, rendering her unable to see where to teleport. That didn't seem to help in this case, though. Ambush Bug teleported willy-nilly, apparently not caring where he ended up. And there was no rhyme or reason to his "crimes," making it impossible to predict his next move.

"I wish we could spare some manpower to help you out—"

"Person-power," Iris interrupted him, clearing her throat significantly. Tapping away at a keyboard at a nearby workstation, she didn't even bother to look up.

Barry nodded. "Sorry, yes, of course. Person-power." Back to Joe: "But we have our hands full here, too."

Joe nodded, his expression weary but understanding. "We're doing the best we can. I just wish you hadn't taken Felicity away from us."

With Cisco and Curtis both lost in time somewhere, Barry had asked Felicity Smoak, Team Arrow's resident hacker genius, to join him in Central City and help out. Ambush Bug was a problem, yes, but recovering Cisco and Curtis, then tracking down Anti-Matter Man, ranked much higher on the priority scale.

Oliver Queen—Green Arrow—stepped into the Cortex. "Felicity's flight just landed. She should be here in a few minutes. How'd it go with the Legends?"

Barry shook his head. "No dice." He quickly explained his conversation with Director Sharpe. "We're on our own for this one."

Iris turned away from her keyboard for a moment, worrying at her bottom lip. "You know, Wally—"

"He wasn't on the *Waverider* when it disappeared," Barry assured her. "He was on leave somewhere in the late sixties. He's fine. And once we figure out how to get the others back, we'll get him, too."

"Unless he comes racing through that door on his own," said

Oliver, pointing to the archway that led out of the Cortex and into the rest of S.T.A.R. Labs. "That's possible, right?"

Barry shrugged a little more diffidently than he felt. "Theoretically, yeah. Wally could generate enough speed to propel himself through time and return to the present. But it's not easy."

Even as he said it, he thought about how easy time travel *could* be. There was the Time Courier, of course, but also the amazing Cosmic Treadmill, the device he'd used in the thirtieth century to run to the sixty-fourth century. Those millennia had sped by like leaves blown by a derecho. But Ava Sharpe had been right—even if he had a million time machines at his disposal, they'd be useless if he didn't know when in time to go.

"You know . . ." Oliver stroked his jawline, deep in contemplation. "This is just way too much of a coincidence. Anti-Matter Man attacks, the Crime Syndicate breaches to our world, and the Legends vanish, all around the same time? That's a little much, isn't it?"

Barry started to answer but was interrupted by a burst of laughter from Iris's workstation. She looked up guiltily. "Sorry, guys."

"What's so funny?"

Iris gestured vaguely in the direction of her screen. "I'm searching for anything that might give us a clue as to Owlman's whereabouts here on Earth 1. So, checking for anything out of sorts or out of the ordinary, I just stumbled upon this guy on Twitter who swears he saw Bruce Wayne right here in Central City."

Barry chuckled at the thought of the world-famous Gotham billionaire playboy showing up in Central City without any sort of fanfare. "Yeah, right. Like he was just wandering down Kanigher Avenue?"

"Basically."

"This is all very amusing," Oliver said, "but can we focus?"

"Sorry," Iris muttered.

"Yes, Owlman's out there somewhere." Oliver began ticking off the problems on his fingers as he spoke. "And Cisco and Curtis are lost in the time stream. And we still have to figure out what to do with ten thousand speedsters from Earth 27. And there's the matter of Anti-Matter Man and who set him free."

"Plus, we have to help Madame Xanadu," Barry added. At that very moment, Caitlin Snow was down in the medical lab, running tests. Madame Xanadu had gone into a sort of coma after the death of her Earth 27 doppelgänger. Barry was determined to help her, as she'd helped him when Abra Kadabra had come to Central City.

"There's a lot going on," Oliver admitted. "And we're down two of our best."

"That's why *I'm* here, darling!" Felicity Smoak crowed as she entered the Cortex, dragging a wheeled suitcase behind her. "Consider S.T.A.R. Labs at full geek capacity once more!"

Oliver put an arm around her and squeezed her lightly. Felicity frowned with her eyebrows but embraced him fully, kissing him square on the lips.

"For the record, Green Arrow, *that* is how you say hello to your wife after three days, especially when you vanished into the time stream for a couple of hours." She looked over at Barry and Iris, both of whom were amused. "Am I right?"

"That does seem to be the protocol, Oliver," Iris deadpanned.

"We don't make the rules; we just abide by them," Barry added.

Oliver grimaced slightly and wiped at his lips. "Fine. Can we move on?"

"He's so romantic, and he's my man," Felicity said with a mocking sigh. "Catch me up to speed. No pun intended. Or, wait. Actually, I won't apologize for the pun. Since when did puns become a bad thing? Why is everyone always apologizing for their puns?"

"Iris has the details on the Earth 27 speedsters and the parameters for the Owlman search," Oliver told her. "And Barry and I are trying to figure out the—"

A loud alert sounded. Iris startled and spun back to her console.

"What's that?" Felicity asked.

"Before he got zapped into the time stream," Barry told her, "Cisco set up some equipment to monitor Anti-Matter Man's unique quantum signature. We've been running it through S.T.A.R. Labs' satellites to make sure he doesn't pop up somewhere else."

"Uh-oh," Iris said, scanning the readout on her monitor. "This isn't good."

"He's back?" Oliver marched over to the console. "Am I going to have to fix this *again*?"

Iris shook her head. "No. Cisco must have patched his system through the breach equipment in the Multiverse lab. We're following Anti-Matter Man through the entire Multiverse."

Felicity sucked in a shocked breath. Barry zipped to Iris's side.

She was right. The display showed Anti-Matter Man currently on Earth 27, the world he'd utterly destroyed. But according to the readout, a breach had opened there, one that led to . . .

"Earth 38," Barry whispered.

Supergirl. Alex Danvers. Winn Schott and all the others . . . They were all in desperate danger.

"Get in touch with Supergirl," Barry told Iris. "Tell her I'm on my way."

"*We're* on *our* way," Oliver insisted.

Barry hesitated. "Oliver, this is—"

"This is big cosmic stuff and I'm a guy with a bow and arrow," Oliver said. "I know. But you needed me last time and you'll need me again."

Barry glanced over Oliver's shoulder. Felicity, gnawing at a knuckle, nodded, her eyes wide with concern, but her expression resolute.

"OK, then. We go together."

The first and last time Oliver had traveled to an alternate Earth was a few years back, during what later came to be called the Crisis on Earth-X. Being abducted to a world where the Nazis won World War II and America was a fascist dystopia ruled over by his own evil doppelgänger had *not* been fun.

Barry assured him that Earth 38 was different.

They geared up, replenishing Green Arrow's quiver with replacements Felicity had brought from Star City, and loaded the data they'd accumulated from the original Central City breach onto a thumb drive.

"We have the coordinates?" Barry asked, strapping on a quantum-tunneling device, which was now the only way they could traverse the barrier between dimensions to get to Earth 38, since Cisco and his vibe powers were gone.

"Yes." Iris helped him type them into the quantum tunneler's interface. Alex Danvers at the DEO had been very specific about where she wanted the Flash and Green Arrow to breach into Earth 38.

"We'll keep looking for Cisco and Curtis," Iris promised, pressing herself into Barry's arms for a last hug.

Barry, Oliver, Felicity, and Iris had all gathered at the Cortex to say goodbye. Iris and Felicity would keep working on the problems haunting Earth 1 while Barry and Oliver tried to stop Anti-Matter Man once and for all on Earth 38.

"I believe in you," Barry told her. "You'll have it all worked out by the time we get back."

"And when will that be?" Iris asked.

Barry and Oliver exchanged a glance. They both shrugged.

"We shouldn't be long," Barry said.

"That's what you said when you went to Earth 27 that time," Iris reminded him.

"Well, yeah . . ."

"*And* when you ran into the future," she added.

"Good point. Assume we'll be gone awhile. But we'll be back." He held Iris at arm's length, then took her hands in his own and gazed into her eyes. "I'll *always* be back."

Felicity cleared her throat into the romantic silence and stared at Oliver pointedly.

"What?" he asked.

"Aren't you going to promise to be back, too?"

"It doesn't matter what I promise," Oliver said very seriously. "Anything can happen."

Felicity threw her hands in the air in disgust.

"That's true," Iris said.

Barry shrugged and gave her his best grin. "Doesn't matter what happens. I'll always come back to you."

"That's romantic, Oliver," Felicity said.

"That's absurd," Oliver announced. "Come on. Let's get this over with."

3

EMERGENCY! EMERGENCY! SUPER-girl thought with as much ferocity as she could muster. *Scramble a medical unit! Prepare a kryptonite needle!*

She was soaring over the National City skyline, cradling her cousin in her arms. Her super-hearing detected a heartbeat, but X-ray vision couldn't penetrate Kryptonian skin, so she had no idea the extent of his injuries. All she knew was that he was alive and that she had to keep him that way.

Kryptonite needle . . . ? J'Onn's puzzlement came through loud and clear.

For a blood transfusion, Brainy said. *You're bringing Superman to the DEO.*

She didn't have time to respond. The DEO building loomed before her. Supergirl focused her X-ray vision, plotting the quickest path to the emergency medical facility within.

I'm coming in hot, she told Brainy. *Clear the balcony and corridors 12 and 5, or I'm coming through the walls.*

In her arms, Superman muttered something. It was a sign of life but so weak and pathetic that it did nothing to buoy her spirits.

"Hang on, Kal," she said, using his Kryptonian name. "If Lex Luthor and the Galactic Golem and Solaris the Tyrant Sun couldn't kill you, this won't, either. I swear."

But what, she wondered, is *this?* He was *Superman.* She couldn't imagine anything on or off Earth that could hurt him like this. What threat could actually knock him unconscious and leave him near death?

As she swooped low over the balcony entrance to the DEO, she tossed those thoughts aside. Time for them later. When Kal-El was no longer in such dire straits. She saw immediately that Brainy must have broadcast her request to the DEO—she had a clear flight path from the entrance to the medical bay.

Alex was already there, standing by a surgical table, wearing a white smock over medical scrubs. She tugged down her surgical mask as Supergirl slowed to a halt and laid Superman on the table.

"Brainy said it was Superman, but I didn't believe it," Alex breathed. "How am I supposed to operate on *Superman?*"

"You know how." It was Brainy, stepping into the room, dressed for surgery like Alex was. "We use a red solar array to limit his powers so that—"

"No," Supergirl interrupted. "He's too weak. For all we know, his powers are the only thing keeping him alive right now. If we take them away, he could die."

"Kara," Brainy said gently. "It's the only way."

Supergirl pursed her lips. Her chin quivered with raw emotion. She sought out Alex's eyes, looking for comfort and safety there, but her sister could only shake her head.

"Brainy's right, Kara. None of our equipment will work on a powered Kryptonian. We can use a kryptonite needle to give him a blood transfusion from you, but we don't even know if he *needs* a blood transfusion." She gestured to the array of medical machinery around them. "This is all useless if his skin is still invulnerable and we can't look inside him to see what's wrong."

Supergirl clenched her fists. "Either decision could mean Kal dies. What do I do, Alex? Tell me!"

Alex came to Kara's side and hugged her sister briefly. "It's not up to me. *You're* his family, Kara. There's no time to call Lois Lane. It's your decision. Tell me what to do."

"Wait!" a familiar voice shouted. "There's another way!"

Lena Luthor strode into the medical bay as though it were the boardroom of L-Corp, the company she had single-handedly relaunched after its abuses at the hands of her brother, Lex Luthor. With a confident toss of her long, black ponytail, she planted her fists on her hips.

"Lex had equipment that could hurt Superman. It was all he worked on, the entire focus of his life. We can use that same equipment to help him."

"How?" Supergirl asked.

"That sounds like using a bullet to stop the bleeding," Alex said. "Not very effective."

Lena shrugged. "Lex's Gamma Blaster can be retuned to use a lower wavelength. Instead of burning Superman's skin cells, it'll make them temporarily transparent. So you can look for internal bleeding. And I can modify the Void Cannon to create a stasis field rather than accelerate entropy."

Supergirl looked to Alex, who nodded slowly. "It could work. We'll keep him stable while you do that."

"An excellent solution," Brainy said. "I'll help you make the adjustments."

They ran off together and Supergirl turned back to the table. Superman lay motionless, his costume torn, his face covered in soot and ash. While Alex prepped her equipment, Supergirl folded her cousin's hand in her own.

"Stay strong, Kal," she whispered in Kryptonese. "We're going to help you, with all the power of Rao at our backs."

32

It had been hours since the fracas at Governor's Park. James Olsen slumped in a chair outside the DEO medical bay. He was exhausted from helping with the evacuation, and all he wanted to do was go home and collapse in bed. Then sleep for something like eighteen hours.

But he'd been dubbed "Superman's Pal" by a puckish press corps years ago, and while the moniker felt minimizing for something as intense as his friendship with the Man of Steel, he still knew it to be true. Superman had saved James's life any number of times. The least he could do in return was . . .

Was what? Wait around?

He clenched his fists in a worthless, impotent rage. He could do nothing. There was nothing he could do to help Clark, his friend, the man to whom he owed so much.

Lena and Brainy came barreling around the corner just then. "We have it!" Lena shouted.

"It's true!" Brainy crowed. "We have it!"

"Have *what*?" James demanded.

"The solution to all of Superman's problems." Lena held up a slender, transparent cylinder. Within, a very familiar glowing green rock was awash in a swirling rainbow of floating, popping globules.

"Kryptonite!" James almost smacked the cylinder out of Lena's hands. "Get that behind some lead! Are you trying to kill *both* of them?"

"Stand down, Elastic Lad," said Brainy. "This is something new. We call it . . . Kryptonite-X."

"*You* call it Kryptonite-X," Lena informed him. "I haven't settled on a name."

"Then it is Kryptonite-X. First mover advantage." Brainy smiled tightly.

"'Elastic Lad'?" James asked.

Brainy's face contorted briefly into that expression he reserved for moments when he realized he'd inadvertently revealed something about the future. "Never you mind. A temporal faux pas on my part. A jape, if you will. In the meantime, we discovered this formula for Kryptonite-X in Lex Luthor's notes."

"When he was a boy, Lex tried to find a cure for kryptonite poisoning," Lena began.

"I know this story," James said. "Move it along."

If she was hurt by his curtness, Lena didn't let it show. "In later years, when he and Superman became foes, he began

33

exploring ways to make kryptonite *more* potent. But what he discovered was—"

"Kryptonite-X," Brainy supplied with an air of almost smug superiority.

"—this stuff," Lena said emphatically. "It uses green kryptonite as a base, yes, but only as a way of weakening the unique Kryptonian cellular structure enough to make it receptive to the energies in the . . ." She paused and frowned.

"Bubbly, swirly things?" James asked, pointing to the cylinder. It was, indeed, full of bubbly, swirly things.

"A liberal arts description of a controlled ambient radiative Kirby energy phenomenon if ever I heard one," Brainy sniffed.

"You're saying this stuff can heal him, right?" James threw his hands up in the air. "Then why are you standing out here talking to *me*?"

Brainy and Lena exchanged blank looks. Brainy raised an eyebrow.

"He has a point," Brainy conceded.

"Go!" James screamed, flinging his arms in the direction of the medical bay.

Supergirl sat by Superman's side. His skin was warm, but she couldn't tell if that was due to his own blood still pumping or just the transfer of her body heat as she clutched his hand with enough force to pulp a normal human's. Some part of her knew that rather than sitting here, she should be out looking for whoever or whatever did this to him. But she convinced herself that

J'Onn could handle tracking down the source of Superman's injuries. She would join up afterward.

"He's going to be OK," Alex said softly, putting a hand on Kara's shoulder.

"Don't make promises you can't keep," Supergirl said.

Her super-hearing detected the tail end of a squabble out in the hall: Lena and Brainy, talking to James, whose heart rate suddenly spiked as he shouted, "Go!" With a slight tilt of her head, she caught Lena and Brainy as they entered the medical bay.

"Give me good news," Alex said.

"No time for good news," Lena said, moving Alex out of the way. "We have to act. Fast."

Supergirl reflexively moved aside but did a double take when she saw what was quite obviously kryptonite in a clear cylinder in Lena's hands. She would know that sickly green glow anywhere. "Are you crazy?" she demanded. "Are you trying to kill him?"

Brainy gently pulled her away from the bed. "In the words of a respected American law enforcement officer," he intoned, "'Trust me; I know what I'm doing.'"

She was Supergirl. A Kryptonian on Earth, where the lower gravity made her superstrong and able to fly. Brainiac 5 couldn't move her unless she allowed herself to be moved. Now, in this instance, she permitted him to shuffle her off to one side—she'd realized that even though the kryptonite wasn't shielded by lead, she felt no ill effects.

"What is that?" she asked.

"A kryptonite derivative," Lena told her. "It will help him."

Supergirl's eyes widened.

"It's not a miracle cure," Lena cautioned her, reading the glee on the Girl of Steel's face. "His body still has to do the work. But this substance—"

"Kryptonite-X!"

"—will make his body more able to repair itself," Lena went on, with only a mildly scornful glance in Brainy's direction.

"So it accelerates his healing?" Supergirl asked, eyeing the cylinder warily.

"Yes." Lena hesitated. "This was the only sample Lex had available. Once it's used, there's no guarantee we can make more. If you think we should hold off, save it for another time—"

"Not a chance! Do it—save him. Now."

A minute passed after Superman's exposure to the new mineral. Then another. Faster than Supergirl thought possible, the minutes stacked up into an hour.

J'Onn joined them halfway through, phasing through the ceiling and transforming from J'Onn J'Onzz to Hank Henshaw in the blink of an eye. His Martian shape-shifting abilities allowed him to take on almost any form; he'd masqueraded as Hank Henshaw for so long that it felt like his natural form, and he defaulted to it almost unconsciously now. He'd locked down the scene at the park with the DEO, then taken to the skies to try to find out what had hurt Superman.

"But it's a big sky, and it could have happened anywhere," he told them. "I'm sorry, Kara."

"It's OK." She impulsively hugged him. "Thanks for trying."

"Did you look at latitude 39.2341752, longitude −98.397283, altitude roughly 13,000 feet?" Brainy asked.

Everyone in the room went silent for a moment. "Why do you say that?" Kara asked.

Brainy rarely shrugged, but he had a particular way of tilting his head while also arching an eyebrow that had the same sort of disaffected impact. "Once I knew that Superman was in fact the falling object, I was able to use his mass in my calculations, conjoined with the arc tangent of his path through the sky, relative atmospheric density, and other factors to determine the origin point of his troubles."

"Wait a second," Alex interrupted. "You took measurements of all those things at the time?"

"Of course not," Brainy said, offended. "I simply *remembered* them."

"You . . . memorized the entire scene at actual size . . ." Kara prompted.

"Yes, of course," said Brainy. "And then replayed my memory, this time taking necessary measurements."

Supergirl, Alex, Lena, and J'Onn all shared a moment of *wow*. If Brainiac 5 noticed, he didn't let on.

"So . . . you're saying you know where Superman was when he was sent spiraling out of control and down to Earth?" Kara asked.

"When did you figure this out?" Lena wanted to know.

"While we were modifying Lex Luthor's kryptonite, of course. When else?"

Lena coughed with surprise. "You were able to do those calculations in your head at the same time that we were biochemically altering some of the most delicate and complicated minerals in the world?"

Brainy made a small *hmpf* noise, almost inaudible. "I possess a twelfth-level effector intelligence. I can process a dozen independent threads simultaneously with no loss in efficiency. Modifying Lex Luthor's tools required only three such threads." He paused. "I had a lot of spare time."

J'Onn sighed. "Very well, then. I'll go check out—"

"Don't," Kara said, grabbed his wrist to keep him from flying off. "Whatever it was, it was strong enough to hurt Kal-El. Let me scope it out first."

She tilted her head skyward and looked through the ceiling with her X-ray vision. Then, with her telescopic vision, she zeroed in on the patch of sky Brainy had identified with his coordinates. What she saw made her gasp.

The sky at 13,000 feet over Smallville, Kansas, was *torn*. There was no other way to describe it. A jagged gash had shredded open the very air, bleeding a sickly red light into the pale blue sky. Clouds that scudded too close to the rip seemed to blow apart, their edges gone black before they dissipated entirely.

It looked like a nightmare version of the breaches her friends Barry Allen and Cisco Ramon used to traverse the Multiverse and jaunt from Earth to Earth. Where the Flash and Vibe's breaches were smooth-edged and gently wobbled with energies, this one was jagged, its border agitated and sharp, limned with a too-deep crimson.

She narrowed her eyes, focusing more, trying to penetrate into the breach itself. But something in its composition blocked her super-vision, just like the energies coruscating around her cousin's body had prevented her from seeing it was him swaddled in all that smoke and ash.

She quickly filled the others in. "It looks pretty bad," she concluded.

"If whatever's in there was powerful enough to hurt Superman," J'Onn said, "then it's *very* bad."

"Do we think it's from another Earth?" Alex asked.

"Could be. Could also be some other, non-Earth dimension." Supergirl frowned, her eyebrows clustering at the worry line that furrowed her brow. "I'm not going to be dumb enough to go up there without a plan, though. Not if whatever's up there could knock Kal for a loop."

"We have to do *some*thing, though," Lena said.

"Perhaps we could develop some sort of remote viewing apparatus," Brainy suggested. "Something that could monitor this . . . breach from a safe remove, gathering information and intelligence."

Before anyone could react or respond, a slight groaning sound came from the bed. Superman opened his eyes.

It took him a split second to realize where he was and what was happening. He smiled apologetically at Kara.

"Sorry I missed your brunch."

Tears flowed freely; she hugged him tightly.

"Whoa!" Alex said. "Easy on the patient."

"I'm fine, Agent Danvers," said Superman, sitting up slightly to return his cousin's embrace. "Easy, Kara. I may feel like I went ten rounds with Darkseid, but I'm all right."

"I didn't think you would be."

He quickly took in Lena and Brainy, then the cylinder mounted next to his bed, its energy dissipating, the glowing green rock slowly dimming from neon bright to a dull matte finish.

"That looks familiar. An anti-kryptonite derivative?"

"We call it Kryptonite-X," Brainy said with a sly anticipatory glance in Lena's direction. When Lena did not rise to the bait, he continued: "I see you've capitulated to my superior intellect and superior naming skills."

"No, it's just that I realize that insisting on having the last word is, well . . ." She sighed. "It's very *tenth-level* intelligence behavior."

With that—and a wicked grin—Lena turned on her heel and strode out of the room. Brainiac 5 marched out after her, yelling, "You take that back!"

Superman grinned as they argued their way down the hall. "Finally: a Luthor-Brainiac team-up I can get behind."

"What a world." Kara sighed heavily and took his hand. "I'm glad you're going to be OK."

"I'm feeling better and better with each passing second." He sat up a little straighter.

James entered the room and slapped his hands together in delight. "You're OK!" He ran to Superman's bedside.

"Jimmy," Superman said, his eyes lighting up. "Good to see you, pal. I've been in worse scrapes."

"I keep thinking your luck's gotta run out someday," James said as they grasped hands.

"Maybe my luck will, but not my invulnerability." He paused, taking in everyone in the room. "Or my friends. Thank you all."

And then, to the astonishment of everyone, he swung his legs over the side of the bed and stood up with nary a wobble or stumble.

"Superman!" Alex exclaimed. "You shouldn't be standing! You need to rest."

He nodded to her. "I respect your medical expertise, but trust me—I'm fine. I've taken worse hits."

"Speaking of, Kal . . ." Supergirl arched her eyebrow. "What did this to you?"

41

"You've seen the breach?" he asked. When she nodded, he went on: "I was in Smallville, just doing some routine farm upkeep, when I heard . . ." He frowned. "Difficult to describe. It was like an enormous popping sound, combined with the sound of a match being lit. I looked up . . ."

"And the sky was torn open," she finished for him.

"Yes. By the time I got up there, it had already doubled in size. And I can see now that it's even larger. Kara." He put his hands on her shoulders and gazed deep into her eyes. "There's something in there. Something that wants to come through. I tried to go, to confront it, but . . . The energy of the portal . . . It actually *hurt*. And I think the sun on the other side of that breach is red—I felt my powers draining away. And then . . ."

"And then you woke up here," James supplied.

"We need to stop it," Superman said, then winced in unfamiliar pain. Seeing the Man of Steel evince any kind of discomfort was . . . troubling, to say the least. Kara had been hurt before, but she wasn't used to watching her cousin squint and suck in his breath with twinges.

"*We* need you to rest up," she told him. "J'Onn and I will go take care of this . . . *thing*. No matter what it is."

Superman hesitated a moment, then nodded slowly. "Be careful, Kara."

"I don't know how to do anything else," she said with as much assurance as she could muster.

But she knew that if she was about to face something that could knock down Superman, *careful* might not be on the agenda.

4

A BREACH FORMED IN THE CENTER of an isolated room at the DEO. Its blue waveforms shimmered and shivered, and then two figures dropped through.

Green Arrow stumbled to one knee, disoriented by the transmission of his molecules from one vibrational plane to another. Barry helped him to his feet. "You all right? It can be a little tricky."

"I'm fine." Oliver brushed off Barry's hand as he stood. The two of them saw a figure nearby, a man who stepped out of the shadows.

"Welcome," he said, "to the place you call . . . Earth 38? Right?"

They took him in. He was tall and powerfully built, with hair so black that its highlights seemed almost blue in the eerie light of the DEO building. He was quite possibly the most at-ease man Barry had ever seen. He stood with a confidence and a disarming charm that belied the obvious enormity of his powers. Barry swallowed hard, aware that he was in the presence of something—some*one*—truly magnificent. He felt simultaneously awed and completely safe, both sensations at levels he'd rarely experienced in his life.

And then Oliver, of course, had to puncture the moment, like an arrow through a helium balloon.

"Who's this guy," Oliver asked suspiciously, "and why is he wearing Supergirl's costume?"

Classic Oliver Queen. Whenever Green Arrow felt too good, too secure, too *happy*, he had to ruin it. Oliver believed that relaxation was a ninja that sneaked up on you and caught you off guard. And when he was caught off guard, he reacted reflexively and without sympathy.

The man's smile, already broad and relaxed, grew even more. "I'm her cousin. I'm known as Superman here, but you can feel free to call me Kal, if that seems more comfortable for you." His eyes darted back and forth between the two of them. "Flash. Green Arrow. I like the costumes."

"How many 'super'-people are there?" Oliver asked as Barry immediately stepped forward and shook Superman's hand. The grip was somehow strong and comforting at the same time. Barry was keenly aware that Superman could crush every bone in his body to powder in the blink of an eye, but that he was effortlessly controlling his strength. What was it like to live in a body so incredibly powerful, he wondered. What was it like to be able to do *anything*?

"Kara thought it would be best for the two of you to come

through in a private area," Superman told them. "I agree. We're not quite as accustomed to Multiversal travel as you appear to be. We wouldn't want to cause a panic here."

"Where *is* Kara?" Barry asked.

For the first time, a glimmer of doubt and concern flickered across Superman's expression. "She and one of our allies have taken to the sky to confront this creature coming through the breach."

Barry and Oliver exchanged panicked glances. "That's a supremely *bad* idea."

Now Superman outright frowned. "I warned them against doing so, given my own experience with the creature—"

"You fought it?" Oliver interjected.

"Yes. And came away with the scars to prove it." He smiled briefly. "Metaphorically speaking. You're worried about Kara and J'Onn. That's enough for me."

"You barely know us!" Oliver protested.

"Kara trusts you. And I'm a fairly good judge of character." He tapped his left ear. "You have good hearts."

"I don't think he's speaking metaphorically anymore," Barry said.

"Can I show you to the command center?"

With a cheerful grin, he turned and led them away.

"*Can* he?" Oliver whispered to Barry as they watched the Man of Steel's cape swish in his wake. "What choice do we have?"

"He can hear you," Barry reminded Oliver, and then followed Superman down the hall.

• • •

The DEO command center had been cleared of all but the most essential personnel for the meeting of the heroes from two universes.

Barry was thrilled to see Kara's sister, Alex, again but was disappointed to learn that Winn Schott, who'd helped him so much the first time he'd visited Earth 38, was no longer available. "Long story," Alex said.

Instead, he was introduced to a striking woman named Lena, as well as a slender young man with a shock of black hair whom everyone called "Brainy."

"We need to tell Kara and her friend to call off her attack," Barry said. "Now. Can you communicate with her?"

"Why can't we just send him to get them?" Oliver asked, hooking a thumb at Superman.

"My powers are still coming back," Superman said with a note of true apology in his voice. "I wouldn't get there fast enough."

Barry grimaced. Speed was his forte, but flying wasn't.

Brainy stared down at the bank of screens built into the pedestal at the center of the DEO command chamber. It almost seemed as though he caressed the monitors with his gaze. Just when Barry was about to ask what he was doing, the DEO agent spoke.

"Their comms are off-line. No doubt due to interference from the breach and the . . . creature."

"We need another way to get in touch with them," Alex said. "Brainy, you hacked into J'Onn's telepathic channel before. Can you do it again?"

Brainy shook his head once. Curtly. Efficiently. "Not at this distance, I regret to say."

They all looked around the room at one another, with mingled expressions of fear, desperation, concern. "We have to do *something*!" Alex yelled.

"You need an arrow," Oliver said quietly.

Everyone turned to look at him.

5

IRIS WOULD NEVER ADMIT IT, BUT SITTING
across a table from James Jesse was absolutely unnerving.

They sat together in one of the anterooms at S.T.A.R.
Labs, steaming mugs of coffee before them. Caitlin had apparently made a phone call and arranged for a nice Danish platter,
but Iris's stomach was tied up in knots—she couldn't even think
of eating. Not while the man who looked *exactly* like the Trickster gazed at her with no more than two feet of lousy conference
room table between them.

"You're thinking about my evil Earth 1 duplicate, aren't
you?" James said.

"No, no!" Iris lied. "Not at all."

"You're staring at me and not saying anything," he said gently.

Iris laughed hollowly. "I, uh, didn't sleep well last night."

He didn't believe her, but he let it go. "Should we continue?"

Meeting with James was one of ten million things on Iris's
to-do list today. He was the nominal head of the Earth 27 refugees

who'd come through the breach that had almost led Anti-Matter Man to destroy the world. Now there were more than ten thousand Earth 27 denizens trapped on Earth 1, their own world polluted and destroyed. They were currently "housed"—a misnomer if ever there was one—in the local baseball stadium. Iris was coordinating with the city authorities to try to figure out what to do with so many interdimensional refugees . . . all of whom possessed at least *some* degree of superspeed.

And their leader was the Earth 27 version of a man who— on Earth 1—was an insane, diabolical terrorist and murderer. Iris knew intellectually that the man sitting across from her was kind, gentle, and good. But her gut screamed, *Run! Get away from him!*

"We're doing our best to figure out housing for your people, James. The Central City Housing Authority is looking into converting some warehouse space into—"

James wrinkled his nose. "Warehouse space?"

"A temporary measure," she assured him. "Better than camping out on a baseball diamond."

Strumming his fingers on the table, James grimaced, then nodded very, very slowly. "Look, Ms. West-Allen—"

"You can call me Iris."

"—Iris, thank you. Look, we appreciate the difficulties here. And we get that it will take time. But I can't go back to my people, who are scared, who have lost *everything*, and tell them that the people of this world plan to *literally* warehouse them. Like . . . cargo. It's already unnerving enough, being here, where all the good people we remember from our world are evil."

So, they both got to use *unnerving*.

Iris drew in a deep breath and slowly released it. "James, we're doing our best. There's a lot going on. There's close to eighty million dollars in property damage downtown alone from Anti-Matter Man's breach and the chaos caused by the Crime Syndicate when you all came through. Believe me, I know how long each second can be to a speedster—but I promise you we're working as hard as we can, as quickly as we can."

He considered, then nodded. "I believe you, Ms. West-Allen." He caught himself and grinned. It was—here comes that word again—unnerving. She half expected him to whip a lethal joy buzzer out of his pocket.

Instead, he stood and offered his hand.

Iris shook it. She didn't really feel like she deserved his politeness, but she'd take it anyway. It was that kind of day.

So, one item checked off her list. Iris made the rounds, heading down to the Dark Lab, where Barry and Cisco stored weapons and such, confiscated from super villains, in "Danger Boxes" designed to protect the rest of the world from their power. She checked the locks on the Danger Box containing the lasso they'd taken from Superwoman and triple-checked the one holding the ring from Power Ring.

Even through the box, she thought she could feel the pulsating energy of that ring. Barry had told her that the ring exuded bad energy, bad thoughts, bad emotions when he held it. Right now, it seemed as though all that pent-up evil was worming its way through the Danger Box. Almost speaking to her . . .

She made a mental note to have Cisco look into reinforcing the box . . . then cursed herself immediately. Cisco was lost in time. Who knew when they'd get him back? She would see if Felicity could whip something up.

One item crossed off the list—*CHECK ON SUPERWEAPONS*—and one item added. At this rate, she'd never get anything done.

Down an elevator and through a winding corridor, she made her way to the Pipeline. Once upon a time—when S.T.A.R. Labs had merely been a particle accelerator—the Pipeline had acted as a chamber for off-gassed dark matter particles. Now, after a retrofitting by Cisco, it acted as a prison of sorts for the very worst metahumans, the ones they feared Iron Heights couldn't hold.

Like the Crime Syndicate of America, Earth 27's very worst metahumans.

Ultraman was asleep in his cell when she entered. Super-woman ignored her. Power Ring was curled up in a fetal position on the floor of his cell, shivering. Without his ring, he was like a drug addict going through withdrawal symptoms. A flicker of sympathy shivered through Iris. Then she remembered that Power Ring had used his ring to rip air-conditioning units off the tops of buildings and throw them down onto the fleeing crowds on the streets below. So, yeah, he could suffer through his withdrawals a little longer.

In the last cell was Johnny Quick, who had removed his cowl and leaned against the glass on one forearm, staring at her with utter loathing.

She'd been told by Barry what to expect when Quick decided to remove his mask. But she still wasn't entirely prepared.

Johnny Quick. Evil superspeedster from Earth 27. And the doppelgänger for Earth 1's Eddie Thawne, the man Iris had once loved.

Earth 1 Eddie had died years ago, sacrificing himself to save the world from the depredations of the Reverse-Flash. So it was startling to see him again, living, breathing. Even more startling was the look of sheer hatred in his eyes. It was the face of the man she'd loved and lost, twisted with a rage and a vile abhorrence she'd never imagined.

"You," he said, spitting the word. White flecks of saliva speckled the clear thymoplastic between the two of them. "I know you. You're Joey West's kid."

Joey West. What had her father been, on Earth 27? What had *she* been?

"I saw you *die!*" he bellowed, smashing a fist into the glass. It shook but held. "I saw you die! But if I have to kill you again, *I will!*" He slammed both fists against the glass now and howled.

Iris's jaw clenched. Her arms, clutching a smart clipboard, tightened, pressing the clipboard against her chest. She said nothing. She could do nothing but stare at the raving lunatic before her.

"Hey, it's OK," said a comforting voice behind her.

Caitlin Snow had come up behind Iris as she stood there, bearing Johnny Quick's withering assault. She put a hand on Iris's shoulder as Quick ranted.

"You have to remember that he's not the Eddie you knew and loved."

"I'll kill you as many times as it takes!" Quick screamed, pressed against the glass, his mouth running with drool.

Iris made a *hmpf* sound. "Idiot doesn't even understand parallel worlds," she sniffed, and turned away.

As she and Caitlin made their way back along the Pipeline entrance, she consulted her clipboard. "You were the next stop on my little tour today," she told Caitlin. "You texted me that there's some special agent or something who wants to talk to me?"

"He's been coming by every few hours and ringing the doorbell. I think he's with the FBI. Agent Smith."

"Agent Smith?" Iris suppressed a chuckle.

"Yep." Caitlin bobbed her head. "Cisco isn't here to make a *Matrix* reference, so I'll do it for him. Uh . . . Agent Smith is . . . He's . . . Uh . . ." She blew out a defeated breath. "Sorry. I whiffed. I've got nothing. Cisco makes this look easy. Anyway, he's really persistent and I know you have a lot on your plate, but he's outside right now and . . ."

Grumbling, Iris swiped on her tablet to open a channel with the outside, not even bothering to look at the camera feed. All sorts of federal law enforcement personnel had come to Central City to help out with crowd control and speedster wrangling in the wake of Anti-Matter Man and the Crime Syndicate's attack. A whole host of them had never been to Central City before and kept trying to pull rank in order to get a peek inside the world-famous S.T.A.R. Labs facility, home of Team Flash. Iris had better things to do than play docent to curious feds, and she told the man at the door precisely that in no uncertain terms.

"But . . ." he protested, and she cut off the communication feed.

"Well, that's done," Iris said, and checked off *FED AT DOOR?* from her list, then moved down one. "Next up: How's Madame Xanadu . . . doing?"

"She's Xanadu-ing OK," Caitlin said, then winced at the pun. "Oh, I see what you were avoiding there. Anyway, I've been keeping her sedated and she seems like she's finally given in to the meds. She actually slept about six hours last night. Real sleep."

"And that's good?"

Caitlin cracked a grin. "I'm a good doctor, but sleep is even better. I suspect the initial trauma and shock of losing the connection to her dead Earth 27 doppelgänger is beginning to wear off. With any luck, she'll be up and about later today. Tomorrow at the latest."

Iris nodded. "Then maybe she can conjure Cisco and Mr. Terrific out of the time stream and back here, where we need them."

And maybe, she thought, *she can also explain that weird vision I had of Barry.*

"Iris?" Caitlin caught her by the elbow and stopped her. "You OK? You suddenly looked really, really . . . troubled."

Iris blinked a few times and banished the thoughts of the odd dream she'd had. "I'm fine. Let's go check in on Felicity."

6

IN THE SKY ABOVE SMALLVILLE, KANSAS, the breach throbbed and pulsated like a suppurating wound, bleeding not fluids but rather noisome winds and spitting, crackling ribbons of radiation. From ten miles away, Supergirl felt its impact, a mélange of death and decay that befouled the air in every direction.

It's like someone opened a portal into hell, she told J'Onn.

H'ronmeer's realm, he agreed. *I feel heat and cold at the same time. As though the souls of the dead have been yoked to the breath of demons and ride them into our world.*

They paused in midair, hovering ten miles out from the epicenter. Kal had described the breach and its size, but it had grown since then. It was a hundred meters wide and almost as tall, a decaying and corrupt oval splitting open the sky. And within . . .

Do you see it? she asked.

Yes.

Within, a massive figure, larger than any creature she'd ever seen before. It was humanoid and bald, its skin a bluish hue, its face expressionless. Remorseless.

"It's coming through." She was so shocked that she forgot to use the telepathic link. "Alex," she said into her communicator. "It's coming through!"

She was greeted with only static.

We're on our own, J'Onn told her. He turned to her as they floated there and extended a hand. *I am honored to battle at your side. On all days. But on this one in particular. Today we fight not for justice or for peace but for life itself.*

Let's do it, she thought to him, and took his hand.

Together, they flew forward. The creature's hands had come through the portal and now—somehow—gripped the edges. Within, she could perceive its head and its torso, filling the breach. There wasn't quite enough room for it to come through entirely.

Until it began tearing the sky even more.

Her mind rebelled against what she was seeing. It . . . Somehow . . . It was *grabbing the sky*. It was *ripping the world open*. In thin air.

You do a flyby to distract it, she told J'Onn, *and I'll hit it with heat vision when it's not looking.*

Got it. J'Onn broke away from her and dived toward the breach—

—and a burst of static exploded in Supergirl's ear.

It hit J'Onn, too, from what she could tell. He wobbled in the air, adjusted his flight path . . .

"Supergirl! J'Onn! Abort your attack run! Return to DEO!"

"Alex?" Kara hesitated, slowing her flight. After a split-second delay, J'Onn had recovered and now bore toward the breach in a straight line.

Nothing. No further communication.

J'Onn, did you hear that?

Just some static. I'm moving—

It was Alex, telling us to retreat. She wouldn't tell us to fall back unless she meant it.

I'm so close, Kara . . . It was telepathic communication— Supergirl experienced the full weight of J'Onn's elation, his fear, his dedication to seeing the task through. *I'm almost there. I can smell . . . scorched clouds. Oh, gods of Mars! What* is *this abomination?*

Break off, J'Onn! She focused all her emotions and all her mental energies into the telepathic burst.

I have to stop it! He wasn't even really talking to her anymore. He pushed forward, his thoughts washing back through the telepathic connection. *It reeks of evil and hate! I must destroy it!*

Kara pursed her lips in worry, her brow furrowed. J'Onn was older than her. So much more experienced. He had spent literally hundreds of years as the Martian Manhunter, stalking criminal prey on Mars, then fighting the good fight as Hank Henshaw on Earth. With her biological father, Zor-El, dead saving Argo City after Krypton's explosion and her adoptive father, Jeremiah Danvers, missing ever since he'd chosen to betray Lillian Luthor, J'Onn had become her de facto father. Never mind the dramatic differences in age, race, culture, species . . . J'Onn J'Onzz was as dear to her as either of the men who'd helped raise her. She couldn't doubt him, not with the stakes so high.

Or could she?

Must she?

In the end, she had to trust her gut. Her gut and her sister.

Then, without another thought, she pushed her super-speed to its utmost, launching herself forward in the sky, fists outstretched.

Ahead, the breach ground open, pulled apart like hardening taffy in the creature's massive hands. J'Onn was a green speck in the foreground. Rolling waves of hot air disgorged from the breach, buffeting him, rippling his cape. He hesitated a moment, no doubt gathering his courage, plotting the best way to strike the human-like shape within.

That pause was all Kara needed. She pushed her speed even further, zooming closer to J'Onn. Just as his fists clenched and his shoulders bunched in preparation for his attack run, she grappled with him from behind and dragged him a thousand feet straight down in less than an instant.

"Kara!" *Kara!* He was so stunned that he spoke and telepathed to her in the same moment, causing an eerie, warbling stereo effect that scraped her brain like nails on a chalkboard. He struggled against her, his incredible strength threatening to burst her arms open. Kal had once called J'Onn "the most powerful being on the planet." They'd never tested that.

She didn't want to test it now.

Tightening her grip, she suddenly found herself holding

nothing at all. J'Onn had phased right through her arms, spinning around, his face contorted into bemused rage.

"Alex said to abort the mission!" she told him. "Stand down!" For good measure, she thought it as hard as she could, too.

"Alex?" J'Onn said. His expression slackened into something more peaceful. "But I was just about to . . ."

"I know." She drifted over to him and looked up. The hole in the sky was growing. Enormous fingertips, down to the first joint, clutched the sides, straining, pulling. "I know, but we have to trust Alex."

"Back to the DEO, then," J'Onn said, and they flew off together.

"Did it work?" Oliver asked, shading his eyes with one hand and looking up in the sky to the east.

"Yes," said Superman. He was on the rooftop along with the Flash, Green Arrow, and Alex. Like them, he was looking up and to the east. Unlike them, he didn't need to shade his eyes. "I see them about four hundred miles out, heading here. They should be here . . ."

He drifted off for a couple of seconds, and then two dots appeared above the horizon, closing in.

"That's fast," Oliver murmured.

"Not *so* fast," Barry said with only a tiny bit of asperity.

Oliver chuckled under his breath. For the first time, he got it: Earth 38 made Barry Allen feel the way non-metas felt around Barry Allen.

• • •

"How did you get in touch with us through all that static interference?" Kara asked.

Alex pointed to Oliver. "It was Green Arrow's idea. He said we needed an arrow. He was right."

They had convened in the DEO command center, where drone and satellite sensors fed a constant stream of telemetry to the surrounding monitors. Superman, Supergirl, the Flash, Green Arrow, Brainiac 5, J'Onn, and Lena stood arrayed around the central monitoring pedestal, but all eyes were on Alex Danvers as she explained.

"We needed a way to boost our signal so that we could get through the static. We built a signal repeater into a javelin and then Superman threw it halfway across the country so that it could ricochet our signal to your comms."

Supergirl raised an eyebrow as she glanced at her cousin. "Only halfway across the country?"

The Man of Steel smiled back at her. "Don't worry—I'm improving every second. I'll be up to full strength in no time."

"Let's catch everyone up," Alex said, adopting her no-nonsense director of the DEO tone. "Time's a-wasting, and every second we delay is another second that *thing* has, to come through the hole in the sky."

The Earth 38 folks quickly filled Barry and Oliver in on what had happened here: the opening of the breach, the attack on Superman (who looked none the worse for wear, Barry noted), the realization that this was bigger than they could handle alone, even with two Kryptonians and a Martian on hand.

"You said you've encountered this thing, too?" Kara asked.

"That *thing* has a name," Barry told them. "According to . . . Well, according to someone we know, it's called Anti-Matter Man."

No one reacted . . . except for Brainiac 5, who made a slight choking sound and then waved off any possible concern with a curt two-finger slicing gesture.

"Anti-Matter Man, then," said Alex. "What can you tell us about it?"

Barry nodded. Between him and Oliver, they explained what had happened on Earth 1. How the Crime Syndicate had ripped open a breach from Earth 27, a breach that had spilled out thousands of superspeedsters. A breach that had given them a window into the blasted, denuded landscape that was now Earth 27.

"That place is entirely uninhabitable now," said Green Arrow. "And unless we can close *this* breach, he'll do the same to Earth 38."

Amid a general murmur of discontent and worry, Supergirl spoke up. "How did you close the breach on your end?"

Barry sighed a long and suffering sigh. "We beat him before by using a gadget Cisco and Mr. Terrific built into Oliver's arrow."

"Then let's do it again," Superman said.

"Cisco and Mr. Terrific are . . . unavailable," Oliver told him.

"We should be able to replicate anything your team put together," Lena said. She looked over at Brainy, who seemed distracted, staring off into the middle distance. "Brainy? Do you agree?"

"Of course." He didn't so much as *snap out of it* as he blinked exactly once and was immediately refocused. "We'll need to capture quantum data from the breach site, as well as . . ."

"Here." Barry handed over the thumb drive. "This is all the data we collected from the Earth 1 breach site. Should be enough to get you going."

Brainy accepted the drive and held it in his cupped hands for a moment. When no one said anything, Oliver said, "Aren't you going to *do* something with it?"

"I am copying the data for internal collation and analysis," Brainy said.

Barry and Oliver shared a gape-mouthed moment. "For real?" Barry asked.

"Brainy's sense of humor doesn't extend to computer jokes," Kara assured him.

"Untrue." Brainy sounded deeply, fundamentally offended by the very notion that there was something he did not excel at. "I will offer a computer joke now: Have you heard of that new band, 1023 Megabytes? They're good, but they—"

"Later," Alex snapped. "We have work to do."

"Hurry," said Superman. He was staring at the ceiling, profound concern twisting his mien.

Kara focused her X-ray vision and telescopic vision along the same path as her cousin. "Oh no," she whispered.

The breach had widened considerably. Anti-Matter Man's head and one arm had already come through, birthing him into a world that could not afford his presence.

"Work fast," she told Brainy and Lena. "Faster than you've ever worked before."

7

WORK FAST, SUPERGIRL HAD SAID.

So of course Barry had to lend a hand.

He joined Brainy and Lena in one of the DEO's labs and did his best to help out. Barry was smart, but Brainiac 5 seemed a thousand years ahead of him, and Lena Luthor wasn't a whit duller than Brainy. Barry allowed himself to help out on the edges, running computer simulations and fetching whatever the others needed in order to do their jobs.

Oliver ambled into the room at one point. "I'm feeling a little useless here," he confided to Barry. "Maybe I shouldn't have come."

"This is going to be all hands on deck time again," Barry told him. "I'm glad you're here. Really."

"Am I going to have to fire another perfect shot?" Oliver asked with only a trace of sarcasm.

"I hope not." He indicated Brainy and Lena with a tilt of his head. "These two geniuses seem to be hitting their stride. I think there's a good chance they'll come up with a better delivery method than the one Cisco and Curtis threw together at the last minute."

"Are you saying their geeks are better than our geeks?"

Barry couldn't tell if Oliver was joking or serious. Then again, he usually couldn't tell if Oliver was joking or serious, so he just always assumed *serious*.

"I think they have a whole different setup here, and they have the advantage of knowing more than we did."

As in most rooms in the DEO, this one had a monitor mounted in a corner up near the ceiling, and it was showing a live television feed of a news channel. Someone announced something. Barry would have ignored it, but at the same time, he heard a small gasp from Lena.

She had glanced up at the screen, and she did a double take. "Is something wrong?" Barry asked her.

"No, it's just that . . . my friend Kara is supposed to be reporting on what happened at Governor's Park. They just showed a snippet of the press conference, and I didn't see her there. I hope nothing has happened to her and that she's all right."

Halfway to saying, "But Kara is in the other room right now!" Barry managed to yank his mouth shut. Lena didn't know that Supergirl and Kara Danvers were the same person. He could scarcely believe it. Lena was a Cisco-class genius, if not smarter. How could she miss something so blatantly obvious?

Oliver tugged Barry's elbow, drawing him into the hallway. "You don't see it, do you?"

"See what?"

Oliver's eyes narrowed and he lowered his voice even more, almost below a whisper. "That Lena woman. You can't believe she doesn't see through Supergirl's disguise."

Barry checked over his shoulder that Lena hadn't come out into the corridor. "How could she not?"

With a shake of his head, Oliver clapped a hand on Barry's shoulder. "You've never understood this, Barry: Consider that she doesn't *want* to know."

"Why not?" That made absolutely no sense.

Oliver offered a lopsided, self-deprecating grin. "I know a disaffected rich kid when I see one, Barry. Lena's got money, resources, and demons. Her friendship with Kara Danvers is probably the most normal, grounding thing in her entire life. On some level, she knows she can't afford to lose that. A powerful brain like hers can uncover the truth, sure . . ."

"But it can also *cover* the truth when necessary," Barry whispered. "I get it. Thanks, Oliver."

Back in the lab, Brainiac 5 and Lena Luthor raced against the clock. They had the Earth 1 data about the breach, as well as hastily assembled schematics from Cisco and Mr. Terrific for the gadget they'd built into one of Green Arrow's arrows. The problem on Earth 1 was the same as the problem here on Earth 38: The breach could only be closed from the *other* side. Given the toxic nature of Earth 27, the Earth 1 team had needed a special delivery system to get the gadget into place. Lacking anything truly special, Lena noted, they'd opted for the literally medieval solution of a bow and arrow.

"This isn't a problem for us," Lena commented as she used a nano torch to solder some circuitry. "We should be able just to have Supergirl fly our version of the breach-closer over to the Earth 27 side and use it from there. Her invulnerability should protect her from the effects of that environment, and her super-speed will enable her to get back through the breach before it closes." Lena tapped one immaculately manicured finger against her chin, thinking. "We'll need to take the time-contraction effect into account, though. Green Arrow ended up propelled through time due to his proximity to the explosion. So Supergirl will need to—"

"Not Supergirl."

Lena broke off. She'd been rambling for quite a while. So long that she'd almost forgotten that Brainiac 5 was in the lab with her, working diligently on the other side of the lab bench.

"Not Supergirl?" she asked. "She has the best chance of—"

"Not her," Brainy said, his tone tight and insistent. "We will send J'Onn. Or Superman. Or I will take it myself."

Lena allowed herself the luxury of halting work for a moment. She'd never seen Brainiac 5 so upset before. His face, frozen in a mask of resolution, barely moved as he spoke. "Brainy? Are you all right?"

"I am *fine*, Lena Luthor. Perhaps you should focus on your own well-being in this . . ." He drifted off. And then, with an almost helpless sigh in his voice:

"It is the day," he whispered.

"What day?" Lena asked. "What are you talking about?"

Brainy continued working, his fingers nimbly and perfectly assembling a timing module for the device they were building. Not for the first time, Lena found herself in the position of concealing her awe at his ability to multitask without loss of precision.

"Brainy. Talk to me," she insisted.

Finally, he spoke. Slowly. Haltingly.

"Historical records are . . . imperfect," he began, pointedly not looking in Lena's direction. "But the presence of Anti-Matter Man . . . is a crucial historical marker."

"A marker of what?"

Brainy clicked a cable into place, surveyed his work, and nodded in self-satisfaction. "If all goes according to history, we will prevail today. But Supergirl . . ." He turned away.

"What about Supergirl?" When he didn't answer her, Lena grabbed his arm and spun him around to face her. "What about Supergirl, Brainy? Tell me!"

He still could not meet her gaze. "This is the day Supergirl dies."

Lena goggled at him. "What? Are you serious? Are you sure?"

"In order: The day Supergirl dies. Yes. Yes."

Lena ran a hand through her hair. "We have to do something about it!"

Brainy put the finishing touches on their breach-closer device. "This may help. But no matter what, we cannot allow Supergirl to deliver the device to the breach."

"J'Onn can do it," Lena said. "He can phase. He'll have the best chance to survive, just like the Flash did on Earth 1."

They exchanged a look as they absorbed this. They both knew that the explosive energies released by the breach's disruption could very well impact J'Onn, even in his phased form. Martian phasing was not the same as a speedster adjusting his vibrational frequency.

Still, it was the best chance to save Supergirl from the ravages of fate.

They burst into the command center. Superman stood off to one side with the Flash and Alex, the three of them speaking in soft tones. Green Arrow stood at the command pedestal, leaning over it, staring with something like fury into a monitor.

And Supergirl turned as they entered, her cape swirling, and planted her hands on her hips.

"We have the—" Lena began.

"It's a moot point," said the Girl of Steel. "There's no hurry to close the breach any longer."

"What do you mean?" Lena demanded. "We have to stop Anti-Matter Man!"

Brainy caught on immediately. "We're too late," he said.

"Yes," Kara told them, her lower lip trembling. "He's come through the breach. Anti-Matter Man is here."

8

EVEN BEFORE HE OPENED HIS EYES, Cisco Ramon could tell something was wrong. There was a gentle breeze and the smell of high grass. So very different from the strong wind and fetid reek from the breach at the intersection of Kanigher Avenue and Heck Street.

He opened his eyes. Blue sky above. Soft grass below. The park? Had something happened? Had Barry run him to the park?

No. He didn't have any of the telltale aches and pains that indicated an involuntary Flash-run.

Heaven? Did Oliver miss and now I'm dead and about to finally have my chance with the cheerleading captain from high school? I know she was into me.

Groaning, he sat up. Off to his left, Mr. Terrific was rising up on his knees, grunting a bit and looking around.

"OK, so not heaven," Cisco said.

"What?"

"Never mind."

As he gazed around, Mr. Terrific peeled the T-shaped mask from his face, working it down from his eyebrows, over the bridge of his nose. It wrapped up into a little ball that he tucked into a pocket. "Where *are* we?"

It certainly wasn't the park in Central City. All around them was a never-ending field of tall grass. The sky was impossibly blue, marred only by a few scudding clouds.

"Maybe it *is* heaven," Cisco mused, standing.

"Or maybe—" Curtis cut himself off. "Do you see that?"

Mr. Terrific, shading his eyes with one hand, gazed out in the distance. With his free hand, he pointed.

Cisco followed the gesture. Yeah, there was *something* out there. Something that glinted bright white, almost sparkling in the sunlight.

Without another word between them, they walked toward the glimmer on the horizon. As they neared it, it began to take shape, wider at the base, tapering as it rose into the sky. The sun in their eyes made it difficult to prize out details until they were closer.

At which point Curtis made a mild retching sound. Cisco swallowed hard, his throat working against his stomach.

What had been pristine and white at a distance was, up close, dirty and bloodstained. It was a tower made of skulls, stacked against and upon one another, reaching easily a hundred feet into the sky.

"Bison skulls," Curtis whispered.

"Are you sure?" They obviously were animals, massive and heavy, but Cisco couldn't tell what animals just by looking at them.

"Yeah. I'm sure. I've read about this. The white hunters would come through the plains and slaughter the bison. For fun. And sometimes they just piled up the skulls like this . . ." He shook his head. "Disgusting."

"So, we time-traveled," said Cisco, staring straight ahead at the tower. "Somewhere into the past. Because there wouldn't be a . . . display like this in our time." He said the word *display* with venom.

"*Or* we're in a future where someone has cloned them and hunts them for sport," Curtis offered.

"You think someone *Jurassic Park*'d bison and we're in the middle of it?"

"It's unlikely, yes, but we have to consider all possibilities."

Grunting something noncommittal, Cisco took a moment to brush dirt and pollen off his clothes. He was still wearing his Vibe outfit, which now felt ridiculously out of place, given that he was in the middle of a plain. Superhero fashion definitely jelled in an urban setting, not so much in the countryside.

"So, this is what Central City used to look like." Curtis had his hands on his hips and turned slowly, taking in the surrounding area. He, too, was still decked out in superhero couture, right down to his black-and-white leather jacket with the legend FAIR PLAY emblazoned on the sleeves.

"Uh, what makes you think this is Central City?" Cisco asked.

"We were *in* Central City when Oliver shot that arrow. Clearly, we missed a variable in our calculations and the resulting breach explosion threw us back in time. In *time*. We didn't move in space at all. So we're in the same spot we were in before, right in the middle of downtown Central." He raised his arms in a gesture that took in the entirety of their sight. "Welcome to downtown Central City, historical edition."

"You're a lousy scientist!" Cisco said, chortling. "Yeah, *we* were thrown through time, but the rest of the world stayed exactly where it was. It's like we were picked up and the world kept spinning beneath us. Then we popped out into the past."

He illustrated with a piece of grass and his own fist, placing the piece of grass on the knuckle of his index finger.

"We're the grass. My fist is the world. Watch." With that, Cisco lifted the blade of grass straight up and moved his fist beneath it, then dropped the grass. It landed on the knuckle of his little finger this time. "See how that works? We could be anywhere."

"*I'm* a lousy scientist?" Curtis hooted with derision. "Where did you learn basic astrophysics, a Chuck E. Cheese? If your theory is correct, we'd be rendered motionless relative to the entire universe, not just the world. In which case, the chances are . . ." He stooped to pluck up his own blade of grass, which he balanced on his fist, then lifted, as Cisco had done.

Then he moved his fist away entirely and dropped the grass, which drifted down to the ground.

"If we maintained our position in space in an absolute sense, the odds are the planet would have orbited away from us. We'd be in the middle of outer space right now."

Cisco frowned, considering this. "You may be right. I may be crazy."

"Well, it's a small consolation. We're still stuck, wherever and whenever we are."

They looked around, now peering everywhere but the tower before them. Natural beauty assaulted them in the other directions—the tall grass, a copse of trees in the distance, and the whisper of mountains on the clouded horizon.

But no clues. No hint of help. No way home.

9

JOE WEST GROANED AND RAN A HAND over his head. He wasn't getting any younger, but he'd managed to hold on to his hair. This case, though, was going to have him pulling out every last strand by the time it was over. He could just tell. It was one of those cases.

"Do we have anything?" Joe asked. "Anything at all?"

John Diggle—Spartan—was out in the field, patrolling the streets to keep the gangs of vigilantes from killing themselves or someone innocent. Working in the Bunker with Joe was Dinah Drake, the Star City cop also known as Black Canary, and Rene Ramirez, also known as Wild Dog. They were both solid and dependable, but right now Joe felt like the team needed a genius. One on-site, not available on FaceTime like Felicity was.

"Nothin', hoss," said Rene, leaning back in his chair, his feet propped up on a keyboard in a way that probably would have driven Felicity crazy, had she been there and not in Central City. "This Ambush Bug guy—"

"Ambush," Black Canary said testily. "He's just called Ambush."

Rene laughed. "Not according to *you*."

Dinah groaned and buried her face in her hands. A couple of days ago, when Irwin Schwab, aka Ambush, had begun his "Reign of Error," the local paper had asked Dinah for a quote. At that point, she'd been running on close to twenty-four hours with no sleep. She'd gotten "Ambush" and "Bug-Eyed Bandit" tangled up in her brain and blurted out the name "Ambush Bug" when describing their quarry. The name stuck, much to Dinah's chagrin and Rene's amusement.

"I don't care what he's called," Joe said. "I just want to catch him and go home."

"Well, good luck with that. Dude can just *pop* wherever he wants, whenever he wants," Rene said, almost cheerfully. Thus far, Ambush Bug's crimes had been closer to practical jokes than anything else. No one had died and the most damage caused had been to egos, as when the Bug had teleported into the mayor's office during an important negotiation with the taxi union and dropped a stink bomb on the conference table, then teleported away, yelling, "This deal stinks! I'm declaring an end to this whole paragraph!"

Negotiations had broken down, needless to say.

"You don't have to sound so happy about it," Joe grumbled.

"Hey, we usually hunt these very grim, very brutal killer types," Rene told him. "I'm enjoying this one. No one's getting hurt. It's like a vacation."

"Remind me not to go on vacation with you," Joe told him. "The Bug himself isn't hurting anyone, but indirectly . . ."

In the wake of Ambush Bug's "attacks," citizen vigilante groups had sprung up around Star City, roaming the streets, looking to stop the Bug. And since this was Star City, of course *counter* groups had formed as well, seeking to stop the first groups. Ambush Bug wasn't hurting anyone, but the people trying to stop him and the people trying to stop *them* were causing a lot of damage.

Just then, the main screen lit up with an incoming call. Joe thumbed the Accept button, hoping for news from Felicity.

Instead, the screen lit up with a massive image of Bertram Larvan. Brother to Brie Larvan, the Bug-Eyed Bandit, currently—and probably forever—stuck in a coma. She was the one who'd developed the swarm of robotic bees that Ambush Bug had stolen and combined with his pilfered teleportation technology. Bert had sort of gotten caught in the middle. He hated the police for what he perceived as unjustly harming his sister, but he also didn't want to see innocent people get hurt *or* Brie's legacy used for ill intent. He'd helped her develop her robot bees in the first place, so he was doing his best to help Joe and the others track down Ambush Bug.

And they had to track him down *fast*. Between the Bug's antics and the ever-growing mobs hunting him on the streets, Star City was one flick of a lighter away from going off like a lethal firecracker.

"Detective West," he said. "Can you hear me?"

"Yeah." Joe sighed as he looked up at the big screen. Bert had an annoying way of holding his phone, such that the camera always offered a view right up his nose. "What do you have for me?"

"I'm still trying to figure out a way to track Ambush Bug through his connection to Brie's bees," Larvan said, completely unaware of the rhyme he'd just dropped. Dinah stifled a giggle and Rene outright guffawed. Joe sighed again.

"Did I say something amusing?" Bert was smart and willing to help, but he also had a very long stick planted precisely in the middle of his hindquarters. Still, he was the only one with anything remotely resembling the scientific knowledge to figure out how to track Ambush Bug's swarm of bees or his special suit.

"Nothing," Joe said, waving the others quiet. "There's some, uh, pollen or something around here."

"Oh. Well. I haven't had any luck, but then again, Brie was the real genius behind all this. I just helped her figure out the entomological aspects of the robots. Still, I'll continue going through her papers and see what I can see."

"Thanks, Mr. Larvan. We appreciate your help."

Joe needed some fresh air. He told Dinah and Rene to hold down the fort and headed up to the street level to take a walk around the block. *Fresh air* was more a theory than a reality, though. This was Star City, and Oliver Queen had planted his Bunker in a not-so-great part of town. The smell of engine exhaust and stinkweed greeted him as he stepped outside. Still, it was better than the reek wafted from the endless platters of gas station sushi Wild Dog insisted on eating. The man's stomach had to be made of cast iron.

He took a ramble around the block, trying to clear his head. Everything seemed foggy, and not just from the car exhaust. He'd been pushing himself—hard—ever since Anti-Matter Man so rudely knocked down the wall between this universe and another one. First, crowd control in Central City, now days of chasing a madman here in Star City. It was making the idea of a transfer to Gotham look like a walk in the park.

"Now I know I've lost it," he muttered to himself, turning a corner. "Gotham's like one big city-sized mental institution."

"Joe?"

Pulled from his reverie by a familiar voice, he snapped his head up and said, "Barry?" But it couldn't be Barry because Barry was on Earth 38 and yet—

And yet it *was* Barry. Standing right in front of him, one hand outstretched, reaching toward him. Barry's Flash costume was damaged, torn across the abdomen, one glove completely shredded so that his scraped and bloody fingers showed through. A wild gash ripped open the top of his cowl, and Barry's hair— dusted with dirt and ash—stuck up through it.

"Joe, I'm sorry. I'm going to make it all work out."

"What?" Joe put his hand out, but in that instant, Barry vanished.

Joe stood perfectly still for a long moment, staring at the space where Barry had been. Ever since his son had become the Flash, Joe had gotten used to him disappearing at a moment's notice. But this time was different. No burst of lightning. No sudden out-draft of wind kicking up the leaves and litter lining the curb.

Barry was *there* and then Barry was *not*.

And besides . . . Wasn't Barry supposed to be in an entirely different *universe* right now?

His lips set in a thin, grim line, Joe turned on his heel and headed back to the Bunker.

10

KARA WORRIED AT HER LOWER LIP, her eyebrows knitted together as she listened to Brainy and Lena explain how their breach-closing gadget worked. The technical details got bogged down—of course, since it was Lena and Brainy—but she picked through them for the important bits.

To her left, Alex was conferring with J'Onn. Once upon a time, J'Onn J'Onzz had spent his days as the director of the DEO, pretending to be a human named Hank Henshaw. Nowadays, he spent his time as a private investigator, but he still knew the old protocols and systems from his days as director. Alex had leaned on him and his expertise quite a bit in the moments after their remote drones confirmed that Anti-Matter Man had come through the breach over Smallville.

"Can you handle the science comms?" Alex asked him. DEO headquarters was in chaos, agents running from station to station, confirming satellite data and drone telemetry. Kara tuned out the din of feet on the floor, fingers on keyboards, in order to listen in on her sister and friend.

"I'll coordinate for you," J'Onn agreed.

"Thanks. I have to brief the president."

Kara stepped over to Alex's side. "Is now really the time for that?" Alex, she knew, was no fan of the president on the best of days. And this was nowhere near the best of days.

"Can't say I'm looking forward to it," Alex admitted. "But DEO protocol is clear: On the scale of possible emergencies, this is top-level, designated Crisis Prime by the DEO's standards manual. Briefing the president isn't optional."

"We've all got your back, you know," Kara told her.

"And I've got yours."

The sisters embraced and then Alex raced to her private ready room for the call.

"We take the fight to him," Green Arrow was saying as Kara rejoined the group. "There's no time to waste. Hit him with everything we've got."

"I tried that," Superman said. "It didn't work terribly well. We need to think our way through this."

"You sure you weren't holding back?" Green Arrow immediately challenged.

A series of gasps erupted around the room at Green Arrow's temerity. Superman simply smiled, as though Oliver's implied charge of cowardice was just another bullet that had ricocheted off his invulnerable flesh.

"You're not from around here," Kara said, "so I get that you don't understand. But, Oliver, this is *Superman*."

"You say that as though it doesn't need anything else to back it up," Green Arrow challenged.

Barry elbowed Oliver in the rib cage. "Be cool, Oliver."

Kara opened her mouth to speak again, but her cousin spoke first. "No one should be above questioning. Certainly not Superman. I'm asking you to trust me, Green Arrow—I gave it my all."

The two men held each other's gazes for a moment, Kal's placid and unconcerned, Oliver's intense and focused. In the space of a few seconds, Oliver relaxed, albeit minutely.

"I trust you," he said as though he'd never spoken the words before, but at least he said it.

"There is one thing . . ." Brainy said, then drifted off, glancing with concern at Supergirl.

"What?" she asked.

"Never mind," he said quickly. "I was thinking of something else. Two tracks crossed over in my mind. An unfortunate rarity, ill-timed."

Supergirl shrugged. Barry looked around. He was in a cluster of bodies in the center of the command room. Superman. Supergirl. That odd "Brainy" guy and the brilliant Lena. Green Arrow.

"C'mon," he said. "Look around. Look at who we are. If I know one thing, it's that the people in this group right here and right now have the key to defeating Anti-Matter Man. We have superpowers and geniuses and a tactical wizard at our disposal. Do you really mean to tell me that between all of us, we can't stop it?"

A silent moment passed between them. Then Brainy said, "It is a . . . thorny issue, Flash."

"No kidding," said Oliver. "Look, I get that he's big and he's made out of anti-matter and that this is a problem somehow, but isn't there a way to knock him back through the breach, back to Earth 27? And then close it behind him?"

"We can't touch him," Superman pointed out. "And anything we use to push him just acts as more fodder for him."

"The matter and anti-matter meet and combust," said Lena, "spewing toxins into the air, causing a chain reaction of even more explosions. And thus, more toxins."

"So we're just going to let him destroy this world, too?" Oliver snapped.

"Not on my watch," Superman said.

"Or mine," said Supergirl, clenching her fists. "If matter is the problem, maybe we try generating our own anti-matter? Brainy, could you put together some kind of . . . I don't know—anti-matter cannon that could do what Green Arrow suggested and knock him back through the breach?"

Brainy had been staring into the middle distance. He shivered a bit and threw off whatever had been distracting him. "What? Oh, hmm, yes, that's a possibility . . ." He wandered off without another word.

"Is he OK?" Barry asked.

"He doesn't exactly seem stable," Oliver supplied, blunt as always.

"This is just his process," Supergirl said, though she didn't seem entirely convinced. "He'll be fine. But, uh, Lena, could you . . . ?"

Lena nodded and ran off after Brainiac 5.

"Is there anything in the Fortress that could help?" Supergirl asked, turning to Superman. "Some sort of weapon or technology you've come across?"

"Fortress?" Barry asked.

"It's just a place I have up north," Superman said. "I keep my stuff there. And I can't think of anything in my inventory that could help us against Anti-Matter Man."

"He has an inventory," Oliver said to Barry. "Now I'm officially impressed."

"You would be." Barry took a third of a second to dash around the DEO, checking every monitor. "Gang, I hate to be the bearer of bad news, but things are getting worse and we're just standing around talking. I get that the rap on speedsters is that we're like hyperactive kids after Halloween, but we have to do *something*."

"That was . . . fast," said Superman, with something almost like awe in his voice. "I could barely keep up with you."

"You saw me do that?" Barry asked, gesturing around the room at the monitors he'd just skimmed.

"We both did," Supergirl said. "We're no slowpokes ourselves."

Just then, Alex hustled over to them. "Have we solved the crisis yet? Someone tell me we've solved the crisis."

"I thought you were briefing the president," Kara said.

Alex shrugged with one shoulder. "I did. He's not a real details guy. More of a passing overview."

"What did he say?"

"And I quote: 'You better damn well save the world, Director Danvers, or I'm gonna tweet something mean about you.'"

"Really?" Barry asked, amazed. "That was the president?"

"Maybe not a direct quote," Alex admitted. "Look, DEO protocol is to establish a remote command center closer to the incident. But we need our lab facilities to work on this, and there's nothing like them in Smallville. We're at a disadvantage because we're not close to the action."

Superman nodded thoughtfully. "I think I can help there, Director Danvers . . ."

11

THE LAST TIME OWLMAN HAD BEEN in a library, it was to burn the place down.

A group of rebels were using the old Bertinelli branch of the Gotham Public Library as a hideout. Ever since Owlman had crushed the pathetic excuse for law enforcement that was the Gotham Police Department and instituted martial law throughout the city, a nagging and annoying band of "resistance fighters" had been a persistent thorn in his side. Led by that do-gooder Anthony Zucco, the group had no chance of wresting control of the city back . . . but that didn't mean Owlman could let it fester.

And so he'd tracked Zucco and his compatriots to their little hidey-hole in the library, and then he'd barred the doors and set the place on fire. Easy-peasy. Done and done. Problem solved.

Now, though, in the North Kanigher branch of the Central City Public Library, he was there to learn, not to burn.

"It's Bruce Wayne!" someone whispered.

Owlman looked up from his computer and smiled at the gaggle of high schoolers standing nearby, all of them clearly too awed and afraid to use the smartphones in their hands to take his picture.

"I get that a lot," he told them. "We just look alike."

That was one of the weirdest things about this alternate Earth he'd ended up on. According to what he could find online, on *this* Earth, Bruce Wayne was some kind of wealthy playboy, a philanthropist with more money than common sense. Known the world over, he was probably the planet's most eligible bachelor . . . and its least intelligent multibillionaire, having inherited his wealth from his parents instead of actually working for it.

Owlman had one thing in common with the Bruce Wayne of this world—they both were orphans. According to the *Gotham Gazette* website and Wikipedia's Bruce Wayne entry, his doppelgänger's parents had been shot to death in an alleyway in Gotham while little Bruce watched.

And yet he grew up to be a feckless imbecile, a useless fop who gives away his money.

Unbidden, Owlman's own parents scrolled through his mind: killed by corrupt police officers in his Gotham City while fighting for justice. Like the Earth 1 Bruce, Owlman had watched his parents die, gunned down by two laughing, carefree cops. Gordon and his partner, Napier. Unlike the Earth 1 Bruce, Owlman had done something about it—when the time came, he had gotten his revenge. Those two were the first cops against the wall when poor, destitute Bruce Wayne grew up to be Owlman, the smartest, deadliest man alive.

The people of Earth 1, as best he could tell, were soft and useless. They survived mainly due to a fluke, a happenstance of fate: Most metahumans on this world had decided to forgo the natural order of things, to coddle and cosset the weak instead of rule over them.

Owlman frowned and kept clicking through the newspaper archives. Unlike the dunderheads in the Crime Syndicate, he understood the values of being patient, of biding time, and of gathering intelligence.

If he was going to conquer this world, first he had to understand it.

12

I'S NOT FAIR TO THE COLOR-BLIND!"
Ambush Bug screamed as he dangled from the cables holding
up the traffic lights at the intersection of Grell and Weisinger
Streets in downtown Star City. Below, traffic snarled. He had a
paintbrush in one hand and a palette of paints in the other. He
was hanging upside down by the crooks of his knees, slapping
bright orange paint on the green light. He had already covered
the red light with a pastel blue.

"Ambush Bug!" Joe shouted, weaving in and out of the
stopped cars, straining to make his voice carry over the constant
bleating of honking horns and commuters yelling in frustration.
"Don't move! You're under arrest!"

Ambush Bug craned his neck, looking for Joe. "Joe! Why
are you upside down? Why is the *road* upside down? My God—
is something wrong with gravity? It's a crisis! Call the Doom
Patrol! Or at least the Teen Titans."

Joe drew his service weapon and aimed at the Bug. "Get down from there right now! I don't want to warn you again!"

The antennae protruding from Ambush Bug's mask quivered. "I'm just trying to make the traffic lights a little friendlier."

"You're gonna cause an accident and get someone killed!" Joe ground his teeth together. He didn't want to fire his gun in the middle of Star City while there were so many innocents around. Yes, he'd be aiming *up*, but if he missed the Bug, the bullet would have to come down somewhere. He'd rather not risk hurting someone.

And if he could distract Ambush Bug just a little longer . . . maybe he wouldn't need to.

"You can't go around painting over stoplights, you lunatic!"

Ambush Bug slapped some paint on the yellow light, turning it white. "I can't? But I just did! Oh, Joe. You're causing some serious cognitive dissonance here. And if I knew what *cognitive dissonance* was, that might bother me."

Joe noticed Wild Dog and Black Canary closing in from two separate angles, each of them out of Ambush Bug's line of sight. Good. Another moment or two . . .

"You have to come down from there!" he commanded the Bug. "Right now!"

"I don't—" Ambush Bug started, and then Black Canary blasted him with her Canary Cry.

The waves of sound were immediate and overwhelming. Joe clenched his jaw and winced in pain. A resounding shout of shock and agony went up from every driver in a hundred-foot radius, as Black Canary's sonic blast rippled forth. Car windows shivered in their slots. Some of them spiderwebbed instantly. It was worth the damage, Joe figured, if he could finally catch the Bug.

Ambush Bug's legs jerked involuntarily and he fell from his absurd perch. Joe ran forward to soften his fall, but at the last moment, there was a soft *pop!* and Joe's arms remained empty.

Another *pop!* Ambush Bug tapped Joe on the shoulder and Joe whirled around. He reached out to grab the Bug, but each time he came close, the Bug would *pop!* a few feet away, carrying on a rambling monologue the whole time:

"Joe! An ambush? After all we've been through? Aren't ambushes *my* deal? I may have to sue you for trademark infringement. Or *someone* could sue you. I am a fully owned and trademarked asset of Warner Bros. Hey, why don't *I* have my own show on the CW? Get Berlanti and Ogawa on the phone, stat!"

"What are you talking about?" Joe yelled in frustration. By now, Black Canary and Wild Dog had joined him. Canary's staff kept swinging into empty air with each *pop!* and Wild Dog lurched around as though he'd been hit repeatedly in the head, stumbling from car to car, banging into them as he tried to grab an enemy who kept teleporting from spot to spot, *pop!*ing into existence on the hoods of cars, on nearby mailboxes, on Wild Dog's shoulders at one point.

"You don't get it, do you?" Ambush Bug said, holding on for dear life as Wild Dog bucked fiercely, trying to dislodge the teleporting madman from his back. "You guys think you're the heroes and I'm the villain, but it's really just that I'm having fun and you're boring. That's why you're stuck in a subplot."

With a ferocious growl, Wild Dog pitched forward, throwing Ambush Bug off. The green-suited foe let out a loud, happy *whoop!* sound as he soared through the air, colliding with Joe. The two of them tumbled to the ground as Wild Dog winced behind his mask and called out an apology.

"Sorry," said Ambush Bug, leaning forward on Joe's chest. "I gotta admit, when Giffen's not writing me, I have a hard time understanding myself. But now it's like I understand the structure of reality. And it's like a book. A middle-grade book, really."

"What are you trying to tell me?" Joe demanded, struggling to knock the Bug off him and stand up. Black Canary and Wild Dog were closing in. Just a few seconds more.

"You know," the Bug went on, "like, for ages eight to twelve, but with subtext and in-jokes that adults would appreciate, too. And then I figure, nah, that's just the pizza I ate last night acting up."

With that, he kissed Joe loudly on the cheek, belched prodigiously, then *pop!*'ed away for good.

Later, as things in Star City continued to deteriorate, Joe's eyes went bleary and his vision doubled for a moment. He was back at the Bunker, running on no sleep and bad coffee as he stared at the computer screen before him. He'd never spent so much time staring at screens before.

"I have Larvan coming in on comms," Black Canary said suddenly.

Joe started and reached for his cup of coffee. He quaffed a mouthful, then spat it back out. It was cold and sludgy. How long had he been sitting here?

"Detective West!" Larvan exploded onto the big screen, his nostrils flaring. "I have some information!"

"I hope so," Joe grunted. "We're getting nowhere. We've got a former serial bomber whacked out on an allergic reaction to synthetic bee stings, teleporting around the city causing havoc. We don't know what his motivation is or what he wants because *he* probably doesn't know. He's just like a wind-up truck that a toddler sent barreling into a pile of LEGOs."

"The plural of LEGO is just LEGO," Wild Dog offered from a corner of the room where he was cleaning his disassembled handgun. When Joe, Canary, and even Larvan all stared at him, he became defensive. "What? I know stuff!"

"Bert, please give me some good news." Joe struggled mightily to keep a note of pleading out of his voice. "Give me *something* I can go on."

"I've been working with this Overwatch person in Central City, and I think we've narrowed something down. Ambush Bug can only teleport to where the bees are."

It took Joe a moment to absorb this new information. Black Canary got there first. She leaned over Joe's shoulder and spoke to Larvan on the screen.

"So you're saying that the bees act as targets for him?"

"In a sense, yes. He stole teleportation technology, correct? I believe he must have built it into some kind of subdermal electronics network."

"Subdermal?" Joe and Dinah exchanged a baffled look.

"Means *under the skin*!" Wild Dog shouted over to them. Then: "Seriously! I know stuff!"

"I will never doubt you again," said Joe before turning back to Larvan. "So . . . let me follow this. He builds some teleportation tech into his own body. And he uses the bees like a . . . a homing signal. To figure out where to zap himself."

"That makes a lot of sense," said Black Canary, drumming her fingers on the desk. "Think about it—if you just teleport into a place blind, you could end up inside a wall or a floor. Or surrounded by people with guns. But bugs can go anywhere and they're hardly ever noticed. They can produce feedback. Let him know where and when it's safe to pop in."

"Bees technically aren't bugs," Larvan said with an air of offense. "One more reason why that ridiculous 'Bug-Eyed Bandit' name they hung on poor Brie was so absurd."

"We'll file a complaint with the people in charge of super-villain names," Joe said. He'd meant it as a joke, but as soon as he said it, he thought of Cisco Ramon. Cisco, who was lost somewhere in time. Why did everything have to be so complicated?

"Is there a way to track the bees?" Black Canary asked. "Maybe we could triangulate his position based on the signals from the bees back to the antennae in his suit?"

"Sadly, no," said Larvan. "The first thing he did when he got the bees was change their signal frequency. We have no way of knowing what it is now."

Joe wearily leaned back in his chair, then shot a glance over at Wild Dog. "So? You know anything about *this*?"

Wild Dog shrugged. "I said I know *stuff*, hoss. I got nothin' on this."

"Keep working," Black Canary told Larvan, patting Joe on the shoulder at the same time. "We're not giving up."

13

THE PAST WAS GETTING HOT.

Cisco and Curtis—after some discussion—had decided that standing still and waiting was a poor course of action. They had to do *something*, preferably something that took them away from the disturbing sight of the tower of skulls.

They headed in the opposite direction, moving away from the scene of the slaughter. It turned out that the direction they'd chosen was west—the sun stuck to their backs for part of the walk, then arced straight overhead. Now, after hours, it lay before them, taunting them.

Broiling them alive. Or so it felt. Other than the occasional Joshua tree, there was no shade. Cisco dearly missed skyscrapers. He stripped off his Vibe jacket and tied it around his head to keep the heat off his scalp and the nape of his neck, but he suspected he already had a grade A sunburn settling in.

Curtis had done the same with his FAIR PLAY jacket. They looked absurd.

"So," Curtis said out of nowhere, "with a tower like that, we've got to be in North America. The Plains bison were almost extinct by something like 1890, so we have to be somewhere around there, maybe a decade in either direction . . ."

"And how do you just happen to know so much about bison?"

"One of my PhDs is in historical ecology."

"Of course it is." Cisco cracked his neck to one side, then the other. "Hold up. I want to try something."

He sat down on the lush carpet of grass and closed his eyes. The muscles in his face tightened, then twitched with some sort of effort.

Cisco breathed in slowly though his mouth, then out just as slowly though his nose. In, out. In, out. Reaching with his Vibe powers. Feeling the frequencies of the universe around him.

Looking for a frequency that was the same, but not quite . . .

He had discovered—quite by accident—that he lived in a specific timeline, one in which Barry Allen had chosen *not* to change the past and save his mother from the Reverse-Flash. That other timeline—the one that had experienced something called Flashpoint—still existed, off in its own Multiverse, and so far as Cisco could tell, the only way to contact it was through his powers, interlocking with the powers of the transuniversal version Vibe in that timeline.

But as much as he reached out, "TV Vibe" was not responding.

"I don't know what I hoped to accomplish anyway," Cisco said as Curtis helped him to his feet. "Even if I could contact him through time, space, and more time, it's not like he could do anything for us."

They trudged on in miserable silence for a while longer.

"So," Curtis said, once again out of nowhere, "not to be that guy or anything, but if we don't find some water in about six hours, we're setting ourselves up for a pair of pretty unpleasant deaths. It can take up to a week to die of thirst, during which time we'll be totally helpless. Our tongues will swell in our mouths, we'll lose more than half our body weight, and our brains could possibly rupture in our skulls."

Cisco stomped to a halt. "Man, for a guy who calls himself *Terrific*, you are one heck of a downer!"

Curtis leaned against a tree. "I'm just being realistic. Food is one thing—we're both typically overfed twenty-first-century Americans, so we can survive probably three, four weeks without food. But we need water, especially after all this heat and exertion."

Cisco closed his eyes. He was accustomed to being able to suss out the solution to any problem, no matter how complicated or thorny. He'd built machines to traverse the Multiverse, for God's sake! And yet here he was, stuck in the world's biggest backyard, and Mom was nowhere to be found with a pitcher of lemonade. Or even a garden hose.

"Can you breach us somewhere?" Curtis asked.

Cisco dreaded the question. He'd been thinking of how best to use his powers since they'd first realized that they were trapped in the past. Unfortunately, he couldn't imagine how those powers could help. He needed to know *where* he was breaching, and no matter what year it actually was around 1890, there would be nowhere known to him. Other than some global landmarks that hadn't changed in millennia—the Grand Canyon, for example. And breaching to the Grand Canyon didn't seem like much of an improvement, even assuming that the Grand Canyon was within his range.

He could also breach them to an alternate universe, but the odds were good that any other Earth was just as useless to them at this point in time.

"Whatever *this point in time* turns out to be," he muttered, after filling Curtis in on his thoughts.

"If we knew more precisely *when* we were, would that help?" Curtis asked.

"Couldn't hurt."

Curtis untied his jacket and rummaged in a pocket, producing a handful of wires, circuits, and other electronics. "The remains of the T-sphere we cannibalized to build Oliver's arrow," he explained. "Plus, we still have our phones. Even without a network to run on, they have computational power. Once the sun sets, we can try to use proper motion to determine when we are."

"That's not exactly going to be a precision measurement," Cisco pointed out.

Curtis wiped sweat from his brow. "You got a better idea?"

Cisco pondered. "Depending on the year, maybe there's something I'm familiar enough with that I could breach us to. Something helpful."

"That's exactly what I was thinking," Curtis said. "In the meantime, we have another problem: I'm worried about your water intake."

Stiffening defensively, Cisco crossed his arms over his chest. "Why mine? You think you're tougher than me? You think you can last longer than me?"

With a chuckle, Curtis shook his head. "Let's be honest—we both saw the insides of a lot of lockers in high school. I'm just worried that if we don't get some water in you soon, you'll be too weak to use your powers."

"Oh." Cisco self-consciously licked his lips; they were dry, and his tongue didn't do much to wet them. He was absolutely parched, and the more he tried not to think about it, the worse it got.

"So," Mr. Terrific went on, "I have an idea. It's a little . . . eccentric, but I think it'll work."

"I used to put *a little eccentric* on my business cards, man. What have you got?"

Curtis cleared his throat and pointed straight up.

14

THE SKY ABOVE SMALLVILLE, KAN-
sas, went bloodred the moment Anti-Matter Man
came through the breach and made his presence
fully known on Earth 38. On the ground below, the people of
Smallville looked up and gasped as the late afternoon sky slowly
metamorphosed from blue to red, an uneven wave of color rippling out from the epicenter of the breach.

Anti-Matter Man's mere presence in the positive matter universe of Earth 38 had begun breaking down physical laws, dis-
rupting fundamental forces of nature at the atomic level.

Clouds touched by the fanning-out margins of the tide of
anti-matter corroded instantly to gray, then to black. The sky
took on the mottled appearance of a rotting strawberry.

Thunder growled overhead like a thing alive. Jagged black
spikes of lightning spiderwebbed the heavens, cracking the firmament into a series of shifting panes of broken stained glass.

Thousands of feet in the air, Anti-Matter Man stood on a platform of nothingness, floating as though even gravity had no choice but to bend to his will. He stretched out his arms, and the air molecules around him crackled, spat, erupted, exploded. Positive matter met anti-matter; the result: abject destruction. A wave of destruction rolled out from him, the explosions daisy-chaining each other as they went, each exploding molecule cascading into a group of others that grew and grew.

The air began to curdle and turn toxic.

Standing more than a hundred meters tall, he was visible from the ground much as an airplane can be seen at its approach and descent. He appeared tiny and unthreatening when spied from the Earth's surface.

But everyone knew. The red skies and the thunder and lightning told the tale.

It was the end of the world. Everyone who looked up knew it.

"Superman will save us," some of them whispered. He'd been saving them for a very long time, and they said it to themselves over and over.

Even though, deep down, they knew it wasn't true.

And above, the crimson blotch of sky grew . . . and grew . . . and grew . . .

15

"**D**O YOU READ ME, LENA?" SUPERGIRL asked into her comms.

"Loud and clear, Supergirl."

"Good."

Supergirl took in her surroundings. She hadn't been to Smallville in years. Kal used to bring her here all the time, when his mother was still alive. But when Martha Kent passed away, he'd come out to the old farm less and less.

Now Supergirl was back, only this time she was thirty feet underground, in Superman's old workshop.

"I used this to tinker when I was a kid," he explained to the others as he pulled old tarps off his lab equipment. "We can use it as a base for now. Everything should still be working."

She was there with Kal, of course, and also Brainy, J'Onn, and Barry and Oliver, who gaped and stared around the room. It was a large chamber, chopped and carved right out of the Small-ville soil by Kal's own hands, the walls fused into solid buttresses by his heat vision. The equipment was a mix of Earth technology from a decade ago and Kryptonian technology. It was the precursor to the Fortress of Solitude, buried deep beneath the Kent Farm.

"You *tinkered*?" Oliver said, running his fingers over a bluish Kryptonian crystal cluster. "It looks like you were growing your own science fiction movie."

"This is an atomic collider!" Barry yelped as he dragged a tarp off a piece of equipment. "I've never seen one this small before!"

"Oh, right." Superman smiled with the fondness of memory. "I was trying to build my own time pool. I forgot all about that."

The Flash zipped to the other end of the chamber and yanked on another tarp. This one slid away to reveal a clutch of humanoid figures, stock-still like mannequins. They all wore Superman's outfit and bore his face from when he'd been a teenager.

"My Superboy robots," the Man of Steel said wistfully. "They were supposed to help me fight crime, but they broke down due to air pollution."

"That sounds like a design flaw," said Oliver.

"Yes," Superman said soberly. "Earth's air pollution *is* a design flaw. Well put, Green Arrow."

"I meant—" Oliver broke off at a sound in his ear. The Earth 1 contingent had been given DEO comms buds to wear, and now his was squawking as it connected to the Command Center.

"We have an update," Alex Danvers said, her voice somber.

The Air Force had attempted a sortie against Anti-Matter Man, scrambling fighter jets from the closest airbase. Four jets had managed to lock onto Anti-Matter Man and launch missiles safely. All four had hit the target dead center.

It didn't matter. When the smoke and flame cleared, Anti-Matter Man stood unharmed, still floating in midair like some sort of indestructible soap bubble.

"I knew that wouldn't work," Supergirl grumbled. "If Kal couldn't stop him, what chance did the Air Force have?"

"They had to try," her cousin reminded her. "They can't go down without a fight."

Lena was at the command pedestal, transmitting data to Brainiac 5, who crunched numbers faster than any computer and sent them back to her.

"According to our calculations," Lena said, "Anti-Matter Man will cross the extinction threshold in less than two hours."

Earth's atmosphere had an effective volume of approximately 4.2 billion cubic kilometers. The chain reaction caused by Anti-Matter Man's presence was therefore converting the air to toxins at a rate of . . .

For the first time in his life, Barry decided not to do the math. It was too depressing.

"Two hours," he said.

"One hour, fifty-four minutes, and sixteen seconds," Brainy said.

"To be precise," the Flash joked hollowly.

Brainy tilted his head at Barry. "Hardly. If you want precision,

I could give you the time to the nearest millisecond, but I'm not sure how helpful that would be, given the present circumstances."

"Everyone!" Alex shouted in their ears. "Everyone pick a station and stay with it!" She was talking to the people at the DEO, but they could hear her in Smallville as she called out several agents by name, ordering them to coordinate military and civil defense organizations. There were most likely going to be many, many evacuations necessary, though to where no one could say for sure. Nowhere was safe.

"Brainy and Lena," Alex said after a moment of shouting at her people, "figure a way out of this mess. Somehow."

"All due respect, Alex," Superman said, "but they *did*. It was just too late to close the breach. If I'd been able to hold off Anti-Matter Man for just a few more minutes, it might have made a difference."

"You couldn't have known what he was or what he would do," Supergirl protested. "It's not your fault."

"Wait." Brainy held up a hand for attention. "Speaking of the breach . . . If the Crime Syndicate opened the breach between Earth 27 and Earth 1, then who opened the one over Smallville?"

Everyone stopped to think about that for a moment. Barry felt like smacking his forehead. Why hadn't that occurred to him?

"An excellent question," Oliver said abruptly, before anyone else could answer. "But it's irrelevant at this point. The breach itself isn't the problem. If we defeat Anti-Matter Man once and for all, it won't matter *how* he opened the breach."

"True," Barry said. He looked around Superman's workshop. "We have a good setup here. I think it's time to talk evacuation."

"We can't evacuate the planet," Kara said. "It's impossible."

"I was just thinking the immediate area," Barry said. "Whatever we get up to . . . up there"—he pointed skyward—"could get dangerous. *Probably* will. We should get civilians out of town."

"Good call," said Superman. "I'll start assembling a transport vehicle. If you and Green Arrow could gather people up, we can shepherd them to safety together."

"Meanwhile, J'Onn and I will work with Brainy and coordinate with Lena back at the DEO," Supergirl said.

"Let's do it!" Barry said.

Overhead, the sky was red.

Red sky at night, sailors' delight, went the old bit of doggerel. *Red skies in morning, sailors take warning.*

Well, this sky was red no matter the time of day, and only getting redder. That would be worrying enough, Barry thought as he ran from house to house, if not for the *other* meaning of *red skies* in his own personal lexicon.

Red skies at all, the Flash will fall, he thought mordantly.

One of his very first experiences with time travel had been almost prosaic: a secret vault concealed in the walls of S.T.A.R. Labs, where Eobard Thawne—the villainous Reverse-Flash from the future—had stashed his gear and a computer AI named Gideon. And with Gideon came a hologram of a 2024 edition of the *Central City Citizen*, a newspaper that didn't exist yet, which bore the headline FLASH VANISHES, along with an explanation that there had been a "crisis" and "red skies" and that the Flash had disappeared thereafter.

That story was written by Iris West-Allen.

In the time since, as her life had changed and Iris had decided to devote herself full-time to protecting the innocent by taking control of Team Flash, he'd wondered if perhaps he'd dodged some futuristic bullet. But the hologram was still there when he told Gideon to summon it forth. And the headline still foretold his disappearance. The byline was now for someone named Victoria Vale, but nothing else had changed.

The lyrics change, but the music stays the same, he thought as he ran into the Smallville General Store. It was empty. The people of Smallville were pretty good at following instructions. He and Oliver had broadcast an emergency decree throughout the town, and people were—in well-behaved fashion—streaming out of houses and stores and schools, heading for the transport Superman had arranged.

Barry looked up into the crimson sky mottled with black clouds, riven by the occasional burst of black lightning. A bolt of black lightning had chased him around Central City a few days ago. Only his tremendous speed had saved him.

And yet the lightning didn't frighten him. It was the sky. The red, red sky.

I'm not ready to disappear, he thought. *Not yet.*

Oliver couldn't run at superspeed, but he had a tactician's mind and more than his fair share of stubbornness. He helped guide the fleeing citizens of Smallville, using gentle persuasion, a kind sort of force, and—when necessary—outright threats to keep the lines moving up Main Street and toward the gigantic platform Superman had rapidly assembled at the edge of town. On occasion, he fired a fireworks arrow into the air, hoping to draw people out of their houses and into the street, where they could be guided to safety.

He was working hard, his brow beaded with sweat. An elderly woman clutching her cat stumbled in front of him. Oliver dropped to one knee, caught her by the elbow, and kept her from falling.

"Thank you, young man," she said, and smiled at him.

It had been a long time since anyone had called him *young man*, either in his Green Arrow getup or as Oliver Queen. It rocked him for a moment, and he couldn't figure out why.

As he stood and helped her back into her place in line, he realized why: She was being sweet and polite to him. She assumed that he was doing the right thing, that he had a plan, and that he would save the day.

More, though: She assumed that he was in the same jeopardy as she was. That his life was on the line, too, and that he was still prioritizing her.

But the fact of the matter was that he had a way out. A ready-made disappearing act. A magic trick made of science.

If things got too bad on Earth 38, if Anti-Matter Man prevailed and the planet was doomed, he and Barry could just "transmatter" back to Earth 1, safe and sound. They would live to fight another day.

It was eminently practical. It made perfect sense. He and Barry had the most experience with Anti-Matter Man. If anyone was going to be able to figure out how to stop him before he rampaged through all fifty-two positive matter universes, it would be them. So they needed to survive.

But still . . .

He thought of the grateful, hopeful look in that old woman's eyes.

And a familiar feeling bubbled up in him: an emotional fire he thought he'd stamped out long ago, now suddenly threatening to burn anew from a single smoldering ember.

Oliver felt like a fraud.

16

IN THE SKY ABOVE THE GRASSY PLAIN where Cisco and Curtis had walked for hours, an eagle glided on a thermal, its wings spread gloriously as it sought the movement of prey below.

Suddenly, a loud hum interrupted the bird's hunt. Air currents shifted dramatically and the eagle's lazy glide became a frantic, wing-beating attempt to stay aloft as a hole appeared in the sky nearby.

The eagle drifted down, spiraled away, then soared off to the north, desperate to flee the breach that had opened.

Cisco stepped through the breach and immediately began falling. He screamed unselfconsciously and lustily as he plummeted. There was no one around to hear him, after all. No shame in screaming for your life as you plunge from the sky.

After several seconds of falling, he whipped up another breach, dropped through it, and found himself collapsing to his knees on the ground next to Curtis, who immediately helped him stand.

"I'm never doing that again," Cisco said once he'd caught his breath. "Not a chance."

"Did you keep your eyes open? Did you see anything?"

"I think I have windburn in my eyes." Cisco rubbed at them. "Man, that stings!"

"Did you see anything?" Curtis insisted.

Cisco nodded. "Yeah, yeah. Your idea worked—I got a quick bird's-eye view of the area. It looks like there's a river or a stream or *something* working its way through some trees thataway." He pointed to the south.

Curtis fist-pumped. "Yes! Let's hear it for aerial reconnaissance."

Cisco blinked rapidly, trying to clear his eyes. "Ouch. Let's get going. I want to wash the sky-grit out of my eyes."

Knowing that they had an oasis of sorts waiting for them, they didn't bother conserving energy. Cisco and Curtis practically ran south, heading for the shelter of trees and the blessed promise of water Cisco had spied from above. The tall grasses scraped and dragged at them, but still they ran. Soon, a line of trees hovered into view, tiny and remote on the horizon.

As the sun slowly set off to their right, they closed in on the trees. To Cisco's unpracticed eye, they looked like elm trees, but all that really mattered to him right now was that they were splendidly full and green. Some part of Cisco took note of that, thinking, *Whatever year we're in, it's either late spring or summer.*

His throat burned and his tongue was a dry rasp filling his arid mouth, but now that they were this close, he wasn't about to slow down. Curtis pulled ahead a bit, his longer legs pumping. Cisco tried to put on a burst of speed and realized that he'd pretty much burst all his speed already. This was as fast as Mama Ramon's kid got, apparently.

I gotta start working out. As soon as we get back to the present, I'm joining a gym. For real.

They crashed through the tree line; sticker bushes and brambles dragged at their legs, their waists. Cisco didn't care—he was positive he could hear the burble of water up ahead.

Burble. What a great word. What a terrific word. Maybe the best word in the whole wide world.

Other than *water*, of course. Water was definitely the best word *ever*.

Curtis ducked a branch, which was a good thing because Cisco was so focused that he wouldn't have noticed it otherwise. He juked left and bobbed his head down to avoid braining himself, then pressed on. Curtis had disappeared from view, but Cisco could still hear branches and dry grass crunching under his feet up ahead.

He followed the sound of Mr. Terrific's footsteps until they stopped, then paused for a moment, breathing hard, his lungs expelling hot, dry air, his lips cracked. No more running sounds, but there was that lovely burble . . .

With a cry of triumph, Cisco rounded an enormous tree trunk and parted a thick barrier of overgrowth. There before him lay a muddy, rocky slope, at the bottom of which ran either the world's most ambitious creek or its most pathetic river. Either way, it didn't matter—it was water.

He half ran, half slid down the slope, joining Mr. Terrific, who was down on his knees, palming handfuls of water to his lips. Cisco opted for the direct approach and dunked his head in. The water was only a few inches deep here, but it was blessedly cool on his sunburned face.

They were silent for a while, save for the sound of the brook and their slurping of the cool, clear water. Whenever in history they were, there was no evidence of sewage runoff or toxic waste in the stream. Intellectually, Cisco knew that the world had not always been as polluted as the one he'd been born into. But emotionally, it was a revelation to be able to drink straight from a stream without worrying about toxins or contamination.

His belly full and his throat slaked, Cisco rocked back and settled on his haunches, catching his breath. After a moment, Curtis joined him on the bank of the stream.

"I just hope there were no fish peeing in the water upstream," Mr. Terrific said after a moment.

Cisco gagged. "Dude! Why? Why? Now I'm gonna throw up."

"Don't. You'll be even more dehydrated than before. And a little fish pee never hurt anyone. Look at it this way—I was upstream of you. I probably drank most of it before it could get to you."

Cisco's stomach rumbled, but the water stayed put. "Man, the next time I'm lost in time, I want a new partner."

17

RIS LEFT FELICITY TO WORK ON THE
Ambush Bug problem remotely while also grinding away
on the issue of the Earth 27 speedsters. She headed down
to the medical bay, still ticking off items on her list. FEMA
and the National Guard had the downtown combat zone
well cordoned off and were assessing damage to the buildings
and infrastructure. She still had to figure out a way to track
down the missing—and dangerous—Owlman, but for now
she had to check in on the one bit of good news she'd had
in days.

"Hello," she said as brightly as she could, sweeping into
Madame Xanadu's room. "Dr. Snow tells me that you're feeling
better."

Madame Xanadu was sitting up in her bed, a food tray lying
across her legs. She'd barely touched the food, but at least she
wasn't screaming or weeping or passing out.

"I am . . ." She paused. "I am well. Thank you."

"I think we're the ones who owe *you* the thanks. You did my husband a solid awhile back."

Xanadu nodded, a small, almost imperceptible smile tugging at her lips. "I offered counsel, that is all. It was up to him to take it."

Pulling a chair over to the patient's bedside, Iris sat down and took the gelatin cup off Madame Xanadu's tray. About six months ago, Cisco had figured out a new formula for gelatin, and the S.T.A.R. Labs version was *amazing*. One of these days, Iris was going to start selling it as an auxiliary income stream for Team Flash. For now, though, she raised a spoon and her eyebrow. Madame Xanadu shrugged and nodded her permission.

"Great." Iris peeled the lid off the gelatin. The enhanced blueberry scent that Cisco had infused in the stuff made her mouth water, and she scooped out a perfectly wiggly spoonful of blue goodness. It tasted like cool, fruity heaven. "Look, I know you've been through a lot. But right now, it would be helpful if you could help us locate our missing people."

Xanadu grimaced, shaking her head. "I'm not a parlor magician or a telephone psychic, Ms. West. My powers are substantial, but numinous and subtle."

"It's Ms. West-Allen," Iris informed her.

Madame Xanadu shrugged, as if to say, *I've proved my point.*

"We need to get Cisco and Curtis back," Iris said. "They're lost somewhere in time. I know you can see other worlds—"

"I see through the eyes of my alternate doppelgängers," Xanadu said with an air of gentle reproof. "From one dimension to another. Not through the time stream."

Iris sucked a glob of gelatin off the spoon, then pointed the utensil at Madame Xanadu in a *gotcha* motion. "Ah, but you gave Barry a card here in the present that turned out to open an important door in the future. The really *far* future." Barry had told her how the mysterious blank card from Madame Xanadu had turned out to open the Spire of the Techno-Magicians in the sixty-fourth century. Without it, he'd have been unable to stop Abra Kadabra from running roughshod over the people of that era and then returning to the present with his powers at their mightiest.

"I gave your husband a card because it *occurred*, Ms. West-Allen. That card was not a part of my deck. It was . . ." She cast about, seeking the right word. "It was conjured by my magic and the Flash's need, working in concert. It was an instrument of fate."

Iris *hmpf*ed.

"I told you my powers were numinous. Ineffable. Even I cannot always explain them." Madame Xanadu stared down at her food tray and picked listlessly at some noodles, stirring them with her fork. "I help those who find me in need. You merely had to walk down a hallway."

"So . . . you're saying that your powers kick in when people stumble upon you?"

"I'm saying that the power of serendipity is a monumental thing, and it enhances my own."

Iris tossed the spoon and empty gelatin cup on the tray, then leaned back in the chair, arms folded over her chest. This wasn't quite working out the way she'd hoped. Then again, Madame

Xanadu's powers were magic. *Real* magic. Scientific laws and rational thought need not apply.

"Can you tell me how Barry is on Earth 38?" she asked.

At this, Madame Xanadu smiled. "I can tell you what my doppelgänger knows. There is danger there. Your husband is in the Midwest, helping people, and the heroes of that world are arrayed against the horror that is Anti-Matter Man, even as the skies turn red."

Iris pursed her lips and nodded tightly. Red skies. She thought of the Time Vault, the newspaper.

Crisis.

18

IN STAR CITY, THEY KNEW NOTHING OF red skies, but they had their own crisis of lunacy and chaos to deal with.

And no leads or ideas until suddenly Joe West shouted, "Wait a second!" and slapped his hand on the table, making Black Canary and Wild Dog jump.

"If you can't figure out the where or the when of a crime," Joe said, his words outpacing his breath, "at least try to figure out the *why*. Am I right?"

Black Canary blinked a few times. "You mean, his motive?"

"He doesn't have a motive," Wild Dog spat. "Dude's *crazy*."

"Wild Dog!" Bertram Larvan, calling in on FaceTime, tsked. "No need for that word. Ambush Bug is suffering from an allergic reaction to the synthetic apitoxin in the robot bees. Saying he's *crazy* connotes that people with psychological or neurological conditions are in some way fundamentally flawed. In point of fact, people with mental health issues are more likely to be victims of violent crimes than the perpetrators of the same."

Wild Dog snorted. "I ain't saying everyone with something screwy in their head is a bad guy, Doc. I'm saying that this particular bad guy has something screwy in his head."

Larvan opened his mouth and raised a finger in the air, ready to lecture, but Joe stepped in, holding both Larvan and Rene at bay. "We can debate the meanings of words later. I think we all agree that Ambush Bug is acting in a manner inconsistent with what we like to call rational thought, right?"

Larvan nodded grudgingly. Wild Dog shrugged. "Right. Crazy."

"But here's the thing," Joe said quickly, before anyone could interject or protest. "He wasn't *always* this way. You met the guy, right, Bert? Did he seem clear-eyed and sane?"

"I suppose so. I'm not a psychologist or a licensed therapist."

"The guy was a bomb expert for hire," Black Canary said. "He had to be in possession of a sound mind."

"Exactly," Joe said. "So he was sane when he formulated the plan to steal the teleportation tech. Sane when he decided to steal the bugs—"

"Bees."

"—the bees and modify their operating frequency. It wasn't until he was stung that he started, uh, seeing the world differently from the rest of us."

Black Canary's eyes widened. "Oh . . . I see. We know what he's up to right now, but what was his original plan? Before he ended up stung and hallucinating."

Joe snapped his fingers and pointed at her. "Bingo. If we can figure *that* out, maybe we can figure out how to track him down. Or how to lure him to a place where we can take him down."

Wild Dog grinned. "I like what I'm hearing, hoss."

19

TODAY IS THE DAY FOR WHAT?" Supergirl asked.

Brainiac 5 startled and looked up from the computer screen before him. He was texting with Alex with his right hand, mousing around on the screen with the other, and clearly doing something else entirely in his head at the same time.

"The day for . . . ?" he asked. Unnervingly, his hands never stopped—he could "read" data from the mouse's Bluetooth connection, and he didn't need to look at the keyboard in order to text Lena. Kara knew Brainy could multitask like no one else on the planet, but it was still odd to behold. And even odder to carry on a conversation with him while he was doing at least two other things simultaneously.

"You've been mumbling, 'Today is the day,' over and over again. For what?"

Brainy's jaw locked and his eyes darted around Superman's old workshop. "The . . . day . . . to . . . prove myself!" He spoke the last two words in a rush, triumphantly, like a man who has just recalled the lyrics to a song in time to win a karaoke contest. "Yes, the day I prove myself worthy of being called a hero."

"Aw, Brainy!" She chucked him under the chin. "You've proven yourself a million times over. In the future with the Legion and here now. You'll come through. You always do."

Brainy's expression fell. "Supergirl . . . Kara . . . Perhaps I should tell—"

"Hold that thought," she said as her phone rang. The screen showed Lena's face. "Oops. Secret identity time. Sorry."

Turning away from Brainy, she thumbed open her phone. It was just a voice call, so all she really needed to do was project the cadence and tone of Kara Danvers. But so much of her act as "mere mortal Kara" relied on body language and overall mien that she found herself slouching just a bit, bringing her shoulders in so as to minimize her heroic posture. It felt so strange to *be* Kara, in Supergirl's costume. Catching Kal's attention across the room, she thought that maybe they should talk about this sometime. How did he reconcile Clark Kent and Superman so well?

"Hi, Lena!" she chirped into the phone, her voice a bit higher, her tone brighter. "What's up?"

"I just have a moment while I'm waiting for some satellite data, and I wanted to check in with you. I'm worried. I didn't see you at the press conference on TV. Is everything all right?"

"I'm fine!" Kara trilled. "I was totally at the press conference. You know me—I just blend right in with the crowd!" She tittered for added effect. "Everything good with you? I'm seeing reports about some crazy stuff happening in Kansas. Anything I should be on?"

There was silence for just a heartbeat too long. Kara focused her telescopic vision hundreds of miles away, peering through the walls of the DEO to see her best friend. Lena looked haggard, almost strung out. Perched on a lab stool, she rubbed her eyes, which were bloodshot and slightly swollen.

"Things are bad," Lena said at last. Kara could hear the hesitation in her voice and witness it in her expression, even so remote.

Even though she was keenly aware that there was crucial, time-sensitive work to be done here and now, the sorry and regret in her friend's voice pulled her away from Smallville and Kal's old workshop. She'd never seen Lena so bereft.

"Lena, talk to me. It's going to be OK."

Lena shook her head with an uncharacteristic ferocity. "No. No, it isn't. Look, I can't get into details. Not now. I have too much to do and there isn't enough time. But . . ." She drew in a deep, trembling breath. "There's a switch under the left side of my desk in my L-Corp office. Left side, Kara. There's a switch on the right side, too, but don't use that one."

Curious, Kara directed her attention to the L-Corp building. Sure enough, her super-vision picked up two switches on the underside of Lena's desk. She started to trace the wiring to figure out what they did, but Lena kept speaking.

"That switch puts my office into lockdown mode and also opens hidden compartments. There's food and water. An air filtration and recycling system light-years beyond anything the Department of Homeland Security has dreamed up . . ."

As Supergirl, she knew exactly what Lena was worried about—Anti-Matter Man's growing toxicity would eventually render the planet uninhabitable. But Lena was looking out for her friend . . . her friend who she didn't know could breathe the fumes of a volcano without much ill effect.

As Kara Danvers, she had to play dumb. "Lena, what are you—"

"Don't ask any questions, Kara." Shifting her sight back to the DEO, Kara watched as Lena sat up straighter, wiped tears from the corners of her eyes. Her strength returned at the thought of saving her friend. "There's no time. Just go there. My passcode is pi to twelve digits multiplied by Lex's birthday plus my mother's maiden name in all caps. Take James. You'll be safe there."

"Lena, I—"

"Go!"

And then Lena broke the connection. Kara watched as, without hesitation, Lena tucked her cell phone away and returned to her lab equipment.

Kara glanced around the workshop. Brainy had returned to his work. Everyone else had their heads down, focused on the task at hand.

She obviously couldn't accede to Lena's wishes. She needed to be here, on the front line, taking the fight to Anti-Matter Man. And she had to believe that she and her allies would prevail.

Still . . . There was no harm in being safe, right?

She used her DEO-issued comms bud to contact James. He sounded slightly winded when he answered.

"What are you doing?" she asked him.

"Just, uh, running up the stairs to my office. The elevator's out."

Kara skimmed National City with her super-vision until she spotted Guardian, chasing a tall man down an alleyway. "Uh-huh. Right."

There was a pause and then he said, "You're watching me right now, aren't you?"

"Little bit."

"OK, so I'm—hang on . . ."

Guardian turned a corner, dropped to one knee, and fired off a grappling hook from his right gauntlet. The hook wrapped around the fleeing man's ankles, tripping him up and sending him careening into a pile of trash bags with a very undignified yelp.

"Nice catch," she told him.

He offered a thumbs-up to the sky.

She laughed. "I'm not in the sky. I'm about five hundred miles behind you."

Guardian turned and aimed a thumbs-up right at her. She smiled. "What's his crime?"

He strode over to the tied-up man, who foolishly tried to lurch up out of the garbage and take a swing. Guardian easily evaded the punch and delivered one of his own, knocking the man out.

"You," he pronounced, "are looking at a looter."

"Already? The red skies haven't even gotten to National City yet!"

Guardian shrugged. "Word's out on the Internet. And someone has to be the first, right?"

His tone was lighthearted and she was enjoying bantering with him, but Lena's call and the stricken expression on her face still hovered before Kara's mind's eye. "James, in all seriousness . . ." And she told him about Lena's panic room setup.

"I'm not going." James's voice was hard. Final.

"James, you need to at least consider—"

"All I need to do is keep moving and keep breathing. Everything else is optional."

She allowed herself a pause, a moment to let his mounting anger die down. "James, it's already bad. And it might get even worse. There's nothing wrong with taking precautions."

"If it gets worse, this city will need me more than ever," he told her. "End of conversation."

"James—"

Knowing she was watching, he raised a hand to his ear and held it there, hovering. He was showing her that he could rip out his DEO comms bud at any moment and end the conversation.

Kara sighed. She had lost her father and most of her family and friends when Krypton exploded. The idea of losing even more here on Earth clawed at her heart. She was invulnerable to almost everything, but not to loss.

And yet, she couldn't discount James's bravery. She couldn't ask him to betray his own courage and go into hiding while the world corroded into a husk.

"Be safe, Guardian," she said, and then looked away.

"I couldn't help overhearing." It was Kal, suddenly standing by her side, one hand on her shoulder. "Jimmy has always needed to walk his own path."

"His path could get him killed," she whispered.

Superman nodded gravely. "I know. We can't tell them which way to walk; we can only walk *with* them. Our powers are a fluke of nature, an accident of birthright. They don't make us any more inherently right than anyone else. They just make it easier for us to impose our will."

"Which is why we have to struggle *not* to." She covered his hand with her own. Kryptonian flesh was nearly indestructible under Earth's yellow sun, and yet it felt just like human skin. "I know, Kal. That doesn't make it any easier."

"The good news," he told her, "is that Jimmy's been in a lot of scrapes before, and he's always come through. And even better is that I think I'm close to a hundred percent now."

She grinned at him. "I need a little more specificity there, Man of Steel."

He waffled a hand in the air. "Say . . . ninety-six point seven percent."

Kara wrinkled her nose. "OK, I'll allow it. But if you'd been at ninety-six point five, I'd bench you."

"Totally understandable."

They shared a brief smile, then—almost by mutual, unspoken agreement—turned serious. Kal pointed to one of the monitors. "Your friends from Earth 1 have done a good job gathering people up. I'm going to go out and move the transport."

"Where are you taking them?"

Superman pursed his lips, thinking. "There's a spot out in the Nevada desert that I prepared a few years back for something just like this. There's food, water, and shelter. They'll be safe there for a while."

Kara barked with laughter. "You set up a town-sized panic room in the desert? Just in case?"

He grinned at her. "You know, I have a friend who says we should always be prepared . . ." He mimed two pointy ears poking up from his head.

"You sure you can handle the transport?" She arched an eyebrow.

"Ninety-six point seven, remember?" And with that, he sped out the exit and back to the surface, leaving her alone with J'Onn and Brainy.

Hadn't Brainy been about to say something to her before her phone call? She thought so. But he seemed busy now, so she joined J'Onn at one of the monitors. She still thought of him as "Hank" most of the time because—as now—he tended to remain in his human form. But she knew that his Martian heritage was as important to him as her Kryptonian ancestry was to her, so she tried to call him "J'Onn" whenever possible.

"Anything new?" she asked him.

"Nothing," he said grimly, his eyes fixated on the monitors. "The DEO's drones and satellites are pulling as much data as possible, but so far there's nothing that has indicated any sort of weakness or vulnerability."

She put a hand on his shoulder. A simple gesture. But it was contact; it was personal. When Kal had done the same to her moments ago, it had helped her relax and refocus, to set aside some of her concern for Lena and James. Now, she felt J'Onn stiffen at her touch. The opposite of what she intended.

"We'll figure it out," she said. "We always have."

"*Always* only lasts until it becomes never," he told her.

Cocking her head, she asked, "Is that a Martian aphorism?"

J'Onn chuckled low and deep in his throat. "I don't think so. I think I just made it up. But I've lived a long life, Kara—it might be something coming from my subconscious." Grimacing, he gently shook her hand off his shoulder. "We've both lost worlds already. I won't lose another one. I can't."

"It's not going to happen," she assured him.

"But how?" J'Onn asked. "How? There's no way to hurt him, no way to reason with him . . ."

Kara blinked in surprise. "J'Onn . . . I think that's it!"

He regarded her with mild suspicion. "What's it?"

"What you just said!" She clapped her hands together in joy. "Kal tried fighting him. The military tried blowing him up. But no one has just tried *talking* to him!"

J'Onn opened his mouth to speak. Froze. Closed it. His expression was puzzled.

"What if there's something he wants or needs?" Kara raced on. "What if we can figure out a way to convince him to reverse whatever's he's done? Or at least give us a clue how to?"

"But . . ." J'Onn had found his voice. "But he's not a real person. According to Flash and Green Arrow, he's a *weapon*."

"But a weapon that lives," she protested. "He's here for a

reason. Even if someone fired him like a bullet, there was a target. An aim. A purpose. If we can figure that out, maybe we can figure out how to stop him."

J'Onn stroked his chin. "I doubt he conveniently speaks English. But maybe I can get something from his mind. Or what passes for it."

Kara chortled. "Now you're thinking! C'mon—let's go. I'll be your backup."

"No!"

The shout came from Brainiac 5, who stood in a gunslinger's pose at the exit back to the surface. In his hands, he held what looked like a cross between a rifle and a small clothes iron. Only, the whole thing was plated in a shining gold metal, its surface utterly smooth except for a gently pulsating red light along the left side.

"Brainy," J'Onn said, "what is—"

"Supergirl cannot go," Brainy said. "I will not allow it."

Kara chuckled. "Good luck with that."

With a raised eyebrow, Brainy returned the chuckle. Only, his was mirthless and hollow. "I am wielding a nanovibrational hammer. Despite its nomenclature, trust me when I say it is a distance weapon. All I need to do is pull the trigger, and it will use a burst of tachyons to retroactively knock you off your feet before this very moment." He paused. "It is . . . a paradox, yes, but a minor one. The universe . . . doesn't mind. I used it in the thirty-first century to bring down Validus and Ol-Vir during the second war with the Legion of Super-Villains. Trust me when I say it can take down even you, Supergirl."

"I believe you, Brainy," J'Onn said, one hand held out steadily, calmingly. "Let's talk about this."

"Why don't you want me to go?" Kara asked. She figured that she could outflank Brainy and get the gun out of his hands before he pulled the trigger, but there was a chance he might get hurt in the process. She wanted to avoid that.

"I cannot say," he told her, pulling his shoulders back into an almost regal bearing. "You will just have to trust me."

"It's difficult to trust a man with a gun pointed at you," J'Onn commented.

"I am certain you can work through it," Brainy replied.

"I'm going to need more than *trust me*, Brainy," Kara told him. She clenched and unclenched her fists.

Brainiac 5 blinked a few times. Sometimes she thought he blinked just to refresh some database in his head. "We have worked together for years, Kara Zor-El. Have I ever led you astray before?"

"You've never pointed a nanovibrational hammer at me before, Brainy. First time for everything."

He tilted his head in acknowledgment as she sucked in a breath. "Yes, well . . ."

She saw her opening. She struck. Instantly.

Exhaling, she aimed right at Brainy's trigger finger. Her precision-targeted super-breath froze the trigger in place. Brainy's eyes widened and he reflexively tried to pull the trigger, but by then she'd already snatched the weapon from his hands.

"Sprock it!" he cursed as he shook his frozen finger back into some semblance of warmth and life. "Sprocking nass!"

"Language," she tsked. J'Onn had already zipped behind Brainy and grabbed him by the arms, restraining him. "We try to keep it PG around here."

Brainy slumped against J'Onn, his chin on his chest, defeated. "Very well, then. You have left me no choice. I must deploy my most devastating weapon."

Kara tensed. With a millennium's head start on tech, who knew what weaponry Brainy had in his arsenal?

"Fire away," she said with a little more bravado than she actually felt.

Brainy straightened as much as he could, considering J'Onn still restrained him. "I shall now employ . . . the truth."

Kara relaxed the tiniest bit.

"I am loath to reveal that which is history to me and the future to you, but now I feel I must." Brainy drew in a deep breath. "Anti-Matter Man's presence here is a matter of historical record in the thirty-first century. Before you ask, no: History does not record how he was defeated."

"But if there's a record of him being here and there's still an inhabitable Earth in the thirty-first century," Kara said in a rush, "then that means we *must* defeat him!"

Brainy shook his head. "No. It means only that at some point between now and my time, Earth recovers from the damage done by Anti-Matter Man. One thousand years is a long time. Much can transpire in that millennium. But my point, Supergirl, is this: According to history, when Anti-Matter Man comes to Earth . . . that is the day that you die."

Kara's hands convulsed on the weapon she'd taken from

Brainiac 5. Her fingers pressed into its strange metallic surface, leaving ten evenly spaced impressions there. The red light went dark.

"You're lying," J'Onn growled, tightening his grip.

Brainy didn't even flinch at the increase in Martian strength. "My fabulist skills are most impressive, when I have time to prepare. I promise you, Martian Manhunter, that I am telling the truth. Per every historical text I have ever witnessed, this is the day Supergirl dies."

Kara dropped the broken weapon to the floor. She and J'Onn locked gazes. She didn't need telepathy to know what he was thinking—the idea of losing her, a daughter figure who'd come to be dear to him—pushed his patience and tolerance to the limit. He would rather crush Brainy to a pulp than admit that the Legionnaire might be right.

"Let him go, J'Onn," she said quietly.

"He's *lying*!" J'Onn's voice quavered with a note of uncharacteristic desperation. "I can't believe that you'll die today."

Kara thought for a moment, then licked her lips. When she spoke, she spoke to both of them:

"When I put on this cape, I did it to save lives. To make the world a better, more just place. You can't have justice if you're dead. There's no better world if Anti-Matter Man makes everything poison."

"Someone else can take your place in the fight ahead," J'Onn said.

"He's right," Brainy chimed in. If not for the circumstances, it would almost be amusing, the two of them agreeing with each other even as J'Onn held Brainy motionless in a modified head-lock. "Superman has recovered to nearly ninety-seven percent power capacity. And we have the Flash as well."

"You're not listening to me," she told them both. "I wear this"—she tapped the symbol on her chest—"because it stands for hope. And because it was worn by my cousin as he stood for truth and justice. I strive to live up to him and he strives to live up to me. And that way, we elevate each other and hopefully everyone else who fights for the cause of peace. We don't pick and choose our battles. We don't decide to sit out the hard ones because they might be too dangerous. We fight the hard battles *because* they're dangerous. Because we're the ones with the power to do it.

"You say history says I die today, Brainy. Well, history also says that in a thousand years, the world will still be here and there will still be people living on it. Maybe those two things are connected. Maybe my death is what makes this planet still livable."

She drew herself up to her full height and set her lips in a firm line. "If so, that's a sacrifice I'm willing to make."

As she watched, Brainy slackened in J'Onn's arms, defeated. J'Onn stepped back, letting Brainy gradually slump to the floor.

"If you are determined," Brainy said, "then I suppose I cannot stop you. As history would imply."

"Kara . . ." J'Onn stepped toward her, his form flickering and transforming as he did so. By the time he reached her, he was no longer Hank Henshaw—he was the six-foot-six, green-skinned, beetle-browed Martian Manhunter. His voice vibrated on an alien frequency. "Kara, I cannot bear the thought of losing you. But as someone who loves you, I more so cannot bear the thought of asking you to be anything less than true to yourself."

He took her hands in his own, big green ones. A single Martian tear splashed down on the tangle of their fingers.

"You are like a daughter to me. I swear that if you die today, it is only because I've died first."

20

A PART OF OWLMAN COULDN'T BE-
lieve how lax things were on Earth 1. For example, right now he was just walking down a sidewalk
near the local baseball park, the place where the speedsters from
his own world's version of Central City were being housed. He
could approach within a hundred yards of the place before being
turned away by a duo of soldiers in uniform.

It was laughable security for so valuable a resource. More
than ten thousand human beings imbued with superspeed, and
the only thing between him and them was a loose phalanx of
utterly normal soldiers with utterly normal weapons.

Back home, he'd have had such a potent mass of power and
potential sealed behind four-inch-thick titanium doors, and
walls made of reinforced concrete. Double-redundant biometric
security systems.

The people of this world were too free. Too trusting. They

would benefit from a strong hand and a keen intellect to keep them in line.

Just like the people back home. In the Gotham City he'd grown up in, a wealthy enclave of privilege and power built on the backs of the poor and impoverished, like his parents. Tommy and Marta Wayne had never had two dimes to rub together at the same time, but they'd managed—against all odds—to build a good and loving family.

And then some rich folks decided that they needed the land where the Waynes lived. It was a run-down apartment complex, half-eaten by rot and decay, but the rich people just had to have a new convention center *right there* so that they could invite their rich friends from other cities to come see the glory that was Gotham. Tommy had led the residents' fight against the forces aligned against them. And they'd been doing well, with several court decisions coming down in favor of the residents who just wanted to keep living where they'd always lived.

Until the cops got involved. Bought off by the wealthiest 1 percent of the city. They trumped up charges against the Waynes and shot them dead trying to "escape" during an arrest.

Bruce had watched from behind the garbage cans in the alley. And he'd sworn, then and there, that he would never— *ever*—rest until he'd made Gotham into a place where no one would suffer such injustice again.

It took him years of training. Of learning from the wretched scum of the underworld in hellholes like Metropolis and Opal City. But he'd gathered the skills and the knowledge to tear down the golden palaces of Gotham's moneyed elite.

And just when he was ready to start . . . the world changed.

Metahumans. A speedster in the Midwest. A flying man. An impossibly strong woman. A man with a ring that could do anything.

He'd recognized immediately that these four, with their powers and their complete lack of self-control and morality, could cause problems for him. He would have to impose that control, but in such a way as to make them think it was voluntary, that the limits imposed on them had been *self-imposed*.

And so he'd followed their lead, adopting their ridiculous notions of costumes and colorful sobriquets as camouflage so as to walk among them. As Owlman, he was one of them, and he gathered them to form the Crime Syndicate of America. Group psychology was a powerful force—tribal notions are hardwired into the human brain. Once they saw themselves as part of a group, their aggressions and their depredations almost automatically became aimed outward.

With subtle psychological trickery and nigh-imperceptible nudges, he convinced them to split up the country among the five of them, dumping four not-so-bright miscreants into situations that required them to use skills and talents they barely possessed. Running a territory was not simply a matter of issuing orders like a petulant toddler. Running a territory demanded abstract thinking, structural understanding, and patience. None of which were prominent characteristics in the Crime Syndicate's roster.

Except for Owlman.

He let them have New York and Metropolis, Central City

and Coast City. The Plains. The mountains. The deserts and the beaches.

Gotham he'd reserved for himself. And within a year, the city was truly *his*, a kingdom of peace, where any threat to order was instantly and ruthlessly excised.

The Bertinellis and the Zuccos and the Maronis, those rich, legacy broods, were hunted to the last of their pedigree, hanged from the highest parapets of Gotham Tower as a warning.

A warning to *anyone* who got out of line.

He stood outside the stadium, taking in the out-of-shape cops, the pathetic sawhorses that blockaded the entrance, the laughable crime scene tape.

Ten thousand superspeedsters.

With only his own brilliance and his own wherewithal, he'd bamboozled the four most powerful people on his world and turned one of its greatest cities into his own personal demesne.

Imagine what he could do with even *half* of those speedsters.

He offered a smile and a jaunty wave to one of the soldiers standing guard and proceeded to imagine precisely that.

21

JOHN DIGGLE—SPARTAN—HAD SWAPPED assignments with Wild Dog. John was weary and exhausted from patrolling the streets, pacifying the vigilante mobs on the hunt for Ambush Bug's apitoxin-laden blood.

Wild Dog seemed relieved to leave the Bunker; he launched himself onto his motorcycle and took off with nary a farewell wave or glance over his shoulder.

Joe West tried not to take it personally. It was actually very, very easy to do.

He caught Dig up on their progress . . . which didn't take long. Much progress had not been made.

"I assume you went over his hideout with a fine-toothed comb," Dig said.

Both Joe and Dinah offered him a sampling of their most withering glowers. They were cops. They knew how to toss a hideout. They wasted no time telling Dig.

"Whoa! Whoa!" Dig held his hands up, palms out. "I surrender! I didn't mean to offend!"

"There was nothing there except whatever camping equipment he was using to squat, plus the tech stuff he was using to operate on the bees." Dinah had gone out for dim sum and now passed a box of shrimp shumai over to Joe, who plucked a dumpling out with his chopsticks.

"Is that Jade Garden?" Dig asked, licking his lips. "Can I get in on that action?"

"Dim sum is for people who don't ask stupid questions," Dinah said darkly, and then very pointedly ate another dumpling.

Dig pouted and slumped in his seat. "What do we know about this guy? Other than the fact that he's all Ambush Buggy?"

Dinah shrugged and called up an info window on the big monitor, filled with information that Felicity had grabbed before heading to Central City. "Irwin Schwab. Born in Paterson, New Jersey. Enlisted in the Army at age eighteen. Served two tours in Afghanistan, two in Iraq, before being honorably discharged. Disappeared off the map for a few years, then showed up as a key suspect in a Kasnian bombing of the Bialyan embassy. Internet chatter on the dark web shows people referring to him as 'Ambush' at around this time. Mercenary bomber. Next five years, he's all over Eastern Europe, Africa, and parts of Southeast Asia, knocking things down that are supposed to stay standing."

"Good money in serial bombing?" Dig asked.

Joe waffled the hand holding the chopsticks. "Not for this guy. According to the job requests Felicity found, he's at the low end of the scale. Yes, there's actually a pay scale for mercenaries."

Dig leaned back and stroked his chin. "But he's good, right? He took down four buildings here in Star City without even touching the ones nearby. That's skill."

With a deft chopsticks maneuver, Dinah plucked another dumpling from the carton. Dig watched like a dog desperate for a treat as she ate.

"We've been thinking about that," she said between bites. "We think his precision is the problem. Some people want messy. They want casualties. Before he became the Bug, Ambush was neat and orderly. No lives lost. No collateral damage."

"So the people who *want* those things stay away from him and drive his price down," Joe supplied.

"Aw, poor baby." Dinah pouted and knuckled her eyes like a sad toddler.

Dig pondered this for a moment. "So, what you're saying is, this guy needs money."

Joe and Dinah considered. "Yeah. Probably."

"What do we have on his financials?" Dig asked.

Dinah sighed, put down her chopsticks, and called up another screen. "Felicity's hack found a checking account that's almost drained and an offshore account that's empty."

"We figure he uses that one to accept money for his jobs," Joe said.

Dig stood up and leaned in close to the screen, scrutinizing it. "I don't buy it. Larvan paid him in cash, right? Guy at his level, he doesn't want a paper trail. And if he's cash-strapped, he doesn't want to have to pay the wire transfer fees." Dig pointed right at the screen. "Look here."

Dinah and Joe both shifted in their seats and bent toward the screen to see what Dig had identified. It hit Joe first, and he sucked in a long breath.

"He just opened the offshore account a couple of days ago. It's new."

"Right after he got his hands on the bees." Dinah slumped. "He's getting ready for a big money infusion. He's planning on selling the bees. Or was, before he got stung and went insane."

"Bingo," Dig said triumphantly. "And you don't sell big tech like that out of a crummy condemned apartment out by the Glades. You gotta do it somewhere swanky. Before he went nuts, Schwab was precise. Left nothing to chance. I bet before all the stinging went down, he'd already lined up the place where he was going to hold the auction. You find that, you find him."

Joe and Dinah nodded thoughtfully, still staring at the screen.

"So, uh . . ." Dig cleared his throat meaningfully. "*Now* can I have that last dumpling?"

Without a word, Dinah handed over the carton. With an almost giddy smile, Dig tipped the dumpling into his mouth.

22

TOGETHER, THEY SOARED ABOVE the Kent Farm and blasted off into the red sky. Kara was slightly faster, but J'Onn was able to keep up, lagging by just a few feet. He watched Kara's cape ripple in the wind, almost blending in with the vermilion firmament.

Red.

Red like the sands of Mars. The memories hammered at him, almost physical blows. Martians lived lives of much deeper psychic awareness than did Earthlings—memories, thoughts, and notions could take on actual tangible sensations for them. Humans had expressions for this—*On the tip of my tongue. Heartache*—but Martians truly felt it. For them, the pain of memory was not a metaphor.

Kara banked left, arcing toward the spot where Anti-Matter Man abided, seemingly weightless, impervious to gravity. J'Onn could fly, obviously, but something about the way Anti-Matter Man simply *stood* in midair . . . It rankled, almost an obscenity.

The casualness with which the creature ignored the laws of physics . . .

Earth's atmosphere was too damp, too heavy, for someone who'd been born to the sere plains of Mars. Its clouds and water-vaporous barrier blocked out radiation deadly to humans but beneficial to Martians. Living on Earth was a process of constant adaptation. For an Earthling, it would be like learning to live underwater. And yet, he loved his new world. He loved its people in all their messy, chaotic incomprehensibility. Even in their disconnectedness from one another and from nature, there was a nobility at their core, often masked by their struggles. But when it shone . . .

It was a beacon to light up the universe.

He would not suffer that light being snuffed out.

Blackish clouds parted as Kara exhaled her super-breath before them. There, in the caesura formed by the cleaved clouds, stood Anti-Matter Man.

J'Onn tried not to gasp . . . and failed. The creature was truly massive, perhaps the largest humanoid J'Onn had ever beheld. He and Kara floated a hundred yards away, level with the creature's knees—it towered another hundred meters up. Had it even taken notice of them? Were they merely gnats in its eyes?

Is this close enough? Kara asked, drifting to J'Onn's side.

I believe so, he told her.

She took his hand and squeezed, transmitting reassurance. Confidence. Faith. The motion took him by surprise, though it shouldn't have. Kara's empathy was nearly Martian in its depth and breadth.

He gritted his teeth, ready to barge into Anti-Matter Man's consciousness, but instead he beheld only static, erupting all around him. There were thoughts and memories caught in the static, but he could not perceive them straight on.

"There's . . . interference," he mumbled.

"J'Onn? What do you mean by interference?" It was Brainiac 5, chiming in over the comms channel.

J'Onn exchanged a worried look with Supergirl. "I don't quite know how to explain it. It's like static in my mind. Like a radio station that's out of tune."

"Multiversal vibration flux." Brainiac 5 said it calmly and confidently, as though they should all know exactly what he was talking about.

"Guys," Green Arrow said, "we're a little busy with evac. Do we *all* need to be on the science geek channel?"

"Wait!" It was the Flash this time. "Brainy, I think I get what you're saying. Meet me back at the workshop, J'Onn."

23

EVERYTHING OWLMAN HAD LEARNED about this world thus far led him to the conclusion that the epicenter of weirdness, metahuman activity, and super-science was a place called S.T.A.R. Labs. There was one on Earth 27, too, but it had been decommissioned and then converted into a fortress by Johnny Quick.

On Earth 1, S.T.A.R. Labs served as the base for the Flash. Fine. That was where he would start, then.

24

CURTIS AND CISCO STAYED UNDER the protection of the trees as the sun set overhead. Now that his thirst was quenched, Cisco turned his attention to the matter of food. He'd last eaten the morning before he'd been booted out of the twenty-first century. Mad science kept no regular business hours, so even though it had been five in the morning, he'd wolfed down a cheeseburger from the S.T.A.R. Labs cafeteria along with half a bag of Cheetos. Breakfast of champions.

The calories from that repast had long ago been burned up. As Curtis had mentioned, they could survive quite a while without food, but the prospect wasn't pleasant.

There were some nearby bushes that appeared to be flowering with blueberries, but Cisco didn't trust his ability to discern safe from poisonous. The berries glimmered in the leaf-filtered light of the setting sun, mocking him with their deliciousness.

Cisco and Curtis emerged from the trees as the day cooled. A band of red and purple glowed around the sun and distant mountains.

"What's that all about?" Cisco wondered. The rich colors reminded him of the effect of air pollution on sunsets—smog ironically made for beautiful twilights. But they were far from any cities both temporally and spatially. There should have been no smog effects.

"This makes no sense," said Curtis, frowning. "The sky shouldn't be so . . ."

"Beautiful?" Cisco supplied.

"Well, yeah."

They hunkered down at the tree line and watched as the sun set and the sky flamed crimson and lavender. After a while, the gorgeous lights dimmed, the sky darkened, and the moon rose, low and pendulous in the blackening sky. As the night sky was revealed, Cisco caught his breath, sudden tears welling in both eyes.

"My God," he whispered.

"No light pollution," Curtis whispered back with something like awe.

The night sky was alive with stars, more stars than Cisco had ever seen outside a planetarium. There were so many stars, giving off so much light, that the night almost seemed like an afterthought. The speckled sky twinkled and shone with a million brilliant pinpricks. The glowing band of the Milky Way stretched across the firmament, sparkling, pristine, iridescent. It was like a spill of quicksilver across a swath of black velvet.

No light pollution, Curtis had said. In his own time, Cisco knew that the development of electric lighting had changed the way the night sky appeared. When daylight faded and everyone turned on their lights, all that earthbound illumination shone up into the air, blocking out most of the visible stars so that only a smattering remained visible to the naked eye. Astronauts could see this panoply of brightness, but not the poor suckers trapped on Earth. For the first time in his life, he was seeing the *true* night sky, and it was absolutely gorgeous.

"I could stare at this all night, too," Curtis said, "but we have work to do."

Cisco tore his gaze away from the sky and focused on the electronics Curtis had removed from his pockets. He started lining them up on a nearby rock.

"We can see the Milky Way, so we know we're in the Northern Hemisphere at least."

"The bison told us that," Cisco reminded him.

"True."

Together, they connected some of the disused T-sphere components to Curtis's cell phone. The idea was simple—take a high-resolution photo of the night sky, then measure the angles between known stars. Due to something called "proper motion," stars in constellations changed their positions slightly over long periods of time as the solar system wound its way through the Milky Way galaxy. Normally, it would take an extremely high-powered telescope to see these deviations, but they were hoping that the hi-res camera on the phone and the massive computing power of the T-sphere would compensate.

Cisco snapped the picture, then handed the phone over to Curtis, who started mucking around with the other components.

Growing impatient after a few minutes, Cisco asked, "Well, Mr. Wizard, what's the verdict? How far back are we?"

"It's Mr. Terrific."

"I know. I'm making a pop culture reference. It's sort of my thing."

Curtis double-checked his numbers. "There isn't that great a deviation from our present. According to this, we're probably only a century or two back in time. Which isn't much more help-ful than what we already knew." Curtis slumped to the ground, deflated.

The idea of being "only" a century out of his own time tick-led and nauseated Cisco at the same time.

"We're gonna need to be as precise as possible if we want to tell someone how to rescue us," Cisco pointed out. "If we get a message to the present somehow, we'll need to tell them—"

"Cisco!" Curtis said excitedly, grabbing at his elbow. "Krakatoa!"

"Kraka . . ."

Cisco's eyes widened in joy and realization. *Krakatoa!* Yeah, he'd zoned out during history class, but this was *science* history: A massive, *massive* volcanic eruption on the Indonesian island of Krakatoa threw absolutely enormous amounts of volcanic ash into the sky. There was so much junk in the sky, hurled with such incredible eruptive force, that it reached the other side of the world, causing all sorts of strange meteorological phenomena for about a year.

Strange meteorological phenomena . . . like a crimson-and-purple twilight where there shouldn't have been one.

"Krakatoa exploded in 1883," Cisco said. "Right?"

Curtis nodded in excited agreement. "And that fits into the estimate we just made with proper motion—1883 is right around a century and a half before our time."

Cisco whistled. He'd take that. Now they had their temporal location narrowed down to a year or two. It was 130-plus years too early, but a lot better than, say, being stuck back in the Pleistocene or something; 1883 felt manageable. It was about a century and a half too soon for Mama Ramon's little boy Francisco, but there would be towns and cities. *Somewhere*. Bathing had been invented, which was feeling really important as he caught a whiff of his own sweat-infused body odor. And while the food might not be four-star cuisine, it would be a heck of a lot better than trying to teach Anthro the Caveboy how to start a fire in order to fry up that hunk of mastodon meat.

Curtis rubbed his hands together excitedly. "Assuming I'm judging the positions of the stars correctly, then we're west of the Rockies. So the explosion *did* move us in space, albeit not that much, relatively speaking. Now we have to figure out how to get home. There's no technology in this era that can do it—"

"Never fear," Cisco interrupted. "After Barry went walkabout in the time stream awhile back, I started working on an emergency time retrieval protocol. Because I plan ahead like that, yo."

"And you have this device on your person?" Curtis clenched his fists in anticipation.

"Not exactly."

Curtis groaned. "It's a pretty black-and-white question, Cisco. Not a lot of shades of gray."

"I know exactly where it is," Cisco said. "I could put my hands right on it. If, you know, we were in the present. The future. Whichever we're calling it."

At Curtis's groan of dismay, Cisco hurried on: "But look, it's just a matter of communicating with the present—*our* present—and getting them to fire up the—"

"Cisco." Curtis shook his head, his expression doleful. "Get real. We don't even know if there's a present to return to! Oliver fired that arrow and now we're here. For all we know, it didn't work."

"It worked," Cisco said defensively. "We both did the math."

But a part of him—a big part, if he was being honest—went cold at the very notion. He'd never even considered the possibility that Curtis had just suggested. What if the arrow hadn't worked properly? What if they'd screwed up and the future was nothing more than a toxic, uninhabitable wasteland being roamed by Anti-Matter Man, with all their friends dead?

"There were still variables," Curtis reminded him. "Especially on the Earth 27 side of the breach. Who knows what happened? We sure didn't predict this!"

"I concede your point. I also do this." He stuck his tongue out.

"Who can argue with that kind of logic?" Curtis asked dryly.

"Look, it's simple," Cisco told him. "We'll just pull a *Back to the Future* and send instructions to the others in the present. Easy-peasy."

"You see a Western Union office around here anywhere?"

Curtis spread his arms out to encompass the entirety of the world around them. "We could walk for months and never hit civilization."

"Not months," said a new voice. "Maybe a week, if you're fast."

With a high-pitched scream, Cisco startled and jumped behind Curtis, grabbing Mr. Terrific by the arms and spinning him to stand between Cisco and the newcomer, who was breaking through some of the bushes behind them.

The man was a Native American, tall and lanky, wearing a tan, fringed buckskin shirt with a high black collar and buckskin pants. Over his left chest was pinned a shiny tin star, and a gun belt with two holstered pistols hung low over his hips.

"We come in peace!" Cisco wailed.

The newcomer rested his hands on his hips, not far from the grips to his pistols. Then he spat laconically into the bushes, eyed the two of them up and down, and said, almost too casually, "So. You fellas are from the future, eh?"

25

BARRY LEFT OLIVER TO HANDLE evacuation on his own for a moment and zipped back to the workshop. Brainiac 5, J'Onn, and Kara were waiting for him.

"Anti-Matter Man comes from the antiverse," Barry began without preamble. "Which means that he's from a universe with a different vibrational frequency than our own. Usually when someone transitions from one universe to another, their vibrations synch up with the new universe. But since he's composed of anti-matter, I think his vibrations are still partly attuned to the antiverse. That's causing the interference you're experiencing, J'Onn."

Kara and J'Onn both nodded thoughtfully but immediately looked over at Brainy for their cue. The superhero from the future offered a single, curt gesture of agreement. "Flash's surmise seems . . . likely."

"I can stabilize his vibrations, though," Barry went on excitedly, "just by altering the air patterns around him, forcing his body to adapt to the vibrational frequency of Earth 38."

"But you can't fly," Kara pointed out. "And I can't carry you up there, because I have to help stabilize J'Onn while he makes contact."

Barry pondered this. There wasn't time to figure out another solution. "We'll have to call Superman back in."

"No need," Brainy said. "Superman's evacuation work is paramount, and there is another way. Here."

With that, Brainy slid a ring off his finger and held it out to the Flash. Barry took it. It was golden, with a black face emblazoned with a stylized letter *L*. He gave Brainy a quizzical glance.

"My Legion flight ring," Brainy said, as though that explained everything.

Actually, in a way it did.

Despite the dire circumstances, J'Onn couldn't help but crack a grin as he and Kara sped back up into the sky, this time joined by the Flash . . .

. . . who whooped and hollered with sheer delight as he soared alongside them, borne aloft by the thirty-first-century technology in the flight ring.

J'Onn and Kara shared a knowing, almost parental look. They'd both been flying for so long that it had become as second nature as walking or running. The unmitigated pleasure of flight, of the loosening of gravity, of the wind and the sky, had long since faded into mundanity for them. Watching the Flash giggle as he swung into an eddy of air or gasped when he happened to look down reminded both of them of the incredible privilege and joy their power could bring them.

"We're here." J'Onn hated to interrupt the Flash's "joy ride," but they'd ascended to Anti-Matter Man's altitude.

He and Kara, the more experienced flyers, hovered neatly in midair. The Flash wobbled by them, drifting up an additional ten feet before finding control of the flight ring again and lowering himself to their sides, bobbing up and down like a cork in turbulent waters.

"Let's do this," the Flash said.

Barry channeled his thoughts into the flight ring and *ziiiiip!* He was gone, flying in a circle counterclockwise around Anti-Matter Man, moving at something close to the speed of light. Brainiac 5 had assured him that the ring—forged of something called Valorium—would let him fly as fast as he could run. That seemed to be true, as the clouds whipped by, blurring into an endless smear of black against the red sky.

He started vibrating his molecules, shivering against the air itself. His plan was to have the very atmosphere around Anti-Matter Man subtly vibrate at a counter-frequency that would cause him to align with Earth 38 completely, allowing J'Onn to enter his mind.

That was the plan. It was pretty much guesswork and mad science, but then again, that's what a lot of his plans seemed to be these days.

He kept flying. While he was at it, he crossed his fingers. Couldn't hurt.

Holding Kara's hand for strength and support, J'Onn furrowed his brow and raised the index finger of his free hand to his temple, ready to bash down the doors to Anti-Matter Man's psyche, if need be.

Instead . . .

Pain

Question

Pain

Answer

J'Onn's teeth clacked together, straining against the sudden agony of—

—birth—?

Pain

A voice cried out to him, but he was too far from it. Too far and too gone. He was submerged in a viscous fluid that clung to him.

Pain

Memory?

The fluid caressed his raw, naked skin. He could feel himself being built, the cells assembling themselves, drawing crude fuel and material from the surrounding gel, sucking it in through his pores, disgorging it as flesh and muscle to lay upon the framework of bone and tendon.

Pain memory question answer

He moved a hand. The nerves there, exposed, roared with pain. He touched something akin to glass. He was in a tube.

Daring to open his eyes, he was assailed by light, and the fluid smeared his newborn vision, but he could see men out beyond the glass. Men, circling the tube, circling him, speaking . . .

". . . reverse nucleic acids and neuronic . . ."

". . . multidirectional growth enhancement . . ."

"With a specific preprogrammed apocalyptic . . ."

". . . greatest weapon the Weaponers have . . ."

He closed his eyes. Tried to shut himself away from the world and the pain, but the pain was the world and there was nowhere to go, nowhere to hide.

"J'Onn? J'Onn!"

Kara was increasingly worried, bordering on panicked. Shortly after raising his hand to his temple, J'Onn had seized, then dropped out of flight. If she hadn't been holding his hand, he might have fallen more than just a couple of feet before she halted him. But she reeled him in and cradled him in her arms, still drifting a few hundred feet from the hulking, titanic figure of Anti-Matter Man.

Wind whipped at her, tossing her hair, billowing her cape. The air sang with Barry's vibrations.

A quick check with telescopic vision told her that Kal was delivering the population of Smallville to his desert staging area. Oliver was returning to the workshop, where Brainy was poring over a tablet, muttering to himself. Should she take J'Onn back there?

He was so still, his body slack and unmoving in her arms.

If not for the sound of his heart beating—its rhythm so oddly syncopated, so alien and Martian—in her ears, she would have thought him dead.

"J'Onn. It's Kara. Please wake up. Please."

J'Onn opened his eyes again to a burst of light. He thrashed in violent response but was held in place by a series of strong straps across his chest, waist, and legs. A man stood nearby, bald, wearing a translucent yellow visor and a white military jacket.

"You will not understand what I say," said the man, "but I feel the need to say it nonetheless. You are our greatest achievement. Our greatest weapon. Made in our image, the greater to strike fear into our foes. Bringer of chaos! Bringer of death! Destroyer of the plus-matter worlds! And yet . . . And yet they say now that we've made you too powerful. That you are too mighty to use, lest you be turned against us."

The man tugged at his ear in frustration. "They are fools, but I am but one man, and against the voice of the Weaponers, no solitary Qwardian may stand. Not for long, at least. I've come to think of you as my child. Which is emotional pap and absurd nonsense, but at least it is true."

The man peered deep into J'Onn's eyes. "There is nothing in there to speak to. I speak for and to myself. For my own posterity. Goodbye."

J'Onn tried to scream, but he could not so much as whisper. His eyes closed of their own accord and—

• • •

Kara's super-hearing picked up a skip in J'Onn's heartbeat. What was happening? She'd never seen him in such a state before. It had been only a few minutes since he'd gone catatonic, but she had no idea how long it was safe for him to be like this. Or even if he'd already passed some crucial threshold. What if contact with Anti-Matter Man's mind had destroyed J'Onn's own psyche? What if it was already too late and she was wasting time, just floating here in the air, buffeted by the noisome winds blowing from the breach behind Anti-Matter Man, holding the brain-dead body of her mentor, her friend?

No, she thought. *I won't believe it. He's doing something. I just need to give him more time.*

Dark.

It was dark.

The darkness of tombs and wombs, the darkness of the bottom of the ocean, of slumber, of eternity.

J'Onn steeped in the darkness. He did not bother to open his eyes—there was nothing to see. There was nothing to hear, not even his own breath or his own heartbeat.

Time had no meaning. Time was for the living and the light. Time was a trap.

After all time and after no time, then—

A voice. A voice in the dark, like a twisted lullaby, calling him to wake, not to sleep. A voice like oil and gravel.

"They imprisoned you in a moon."

J'Onn's ears roared and burned at the first sound they'd heard since forever ago. He wanted to scream but could not.

"How *mythic*," the voice went on. "They thought this would keep you from the world. They thought too small. And I . . . I thought large. And long."

He did not open his eyes, but he saw nonetheless. Sudden light, strong enough, powerful enough to shine through his eyelids. The first light since the last light.

Now J'Onn opened his eyes to the violence of sight. Enveloped in darkness, a metal coffin around him, one side of it cleanly vaporized. Before him, a swirling red-and-gray cloud rippled and convulsed, exuding a bright, cold light. Within the light, a shadowy figure stood, silent and ominous, its body cloaked, its head hooded.

Then, as his eyesight adjusted to use for the first time in so long, he peered deeper into the bright abyss. A ruined sky of black and blue hovered over a denuded plain, choked with debris and shaken by occasional bursts of dark, throbbing energies. He could see dying stars and shattered planets overhead, and a smear of dirty red light.

There, in the distance, behind the figure, was a massive machine, a nightmarish sort of gyroscope, spinning disks intersecting and grinding against one another, throwing off powerful sparks and coruscating energies.

And at the center of that machinery—a figure moving so fast as to be a blur, its outline barely distinguishable. Arms pumping, legs churning . . .

The cloaked and hooded figure raised a hand and pointed to him.

"Now you are mine. They made you for destruction.

And then they left you. But I have use for you. Speak your name."

And J'Onn opened his mouth and said . . .

"Anti-Matter Man!"

Kara wobbled in midair as J'Onn lurched in her arms, jerking into a sitting position with no warning whatsoever, his eyes wide and glowing. His shape shifted slightly, flickering for a moment into something like Anti-Matter Man before returning to its natural Martian form.

"Anti-Matter Man," he said again. "I am Anti-Matter Man!"

"No!" Kara admonished him. "You're J'Onn J'Onzz. You're Hank Henshaw." She shook him gently, wanting to rattle him, not harm him. "You're my *friend*."

J'Onn's head swiveled as though he were blind, his gaze falling on clouds, lightning, the ground, then finally coming to rest on Kara. The sight of her seemed to jostle him into some sort of awareness. He blinked repeatedly and worked his lips silently, then, finally, said, "Kara?"

She held back tears. "Yes. It's me. You're OK."

J'Onn stroked her cheek lightly with the pads of his fingers. "How . . . how long have I been gone?"

"How long?" Kara regarded him quizzically. "Like, maybe three minutes?"

J'Onn shuddered. With a gesture, he indicated that he wanted to try flying on his own. Reluctantly, Kara let him go, secure in the knowledge that if he fell, she could catch him.

He shook side to side but managed to remain airborne. In the next heartbeat, the wind died down a bit and Barry—clearly dizzy from his exertions—came to a rest nearby.

"How'd it go?" the Flash asked. "Did I get airsick for nothing?"

"We need to talk to the others," J'Onn told them, his voice gaining strength. "We need to do it *now*."

26

WE THINK WE HAVE A LEAD," JOE told Iris. They were FaceTiming as Iris wolfed down a lunch of microwaveable pizza and Skittles in between dealing with the usual crises du jour. "We're searching some of the high-end hotels and Airbnbs for a Schwab reservation."

"Tell her it was my idea!" Diggle shouted from off-screen.

"I'm wondering," Joe went on, ignoring Dig, "if Felicity could spare five minutes—"

"—to hack into the reservation databases and take a look-see?" Iris finished for him. "Sure. I'll talk to her."

"Thanks, baby." Joe's brow furrowed with fatherly concern. "Are you eating Skittles by the handful?"

"I need the sugar rush, Dad. Don't you dare judge me. I've watched you guzzle coffee straight from the urn when you were on a hot case."

Joe held up his free hand in apology. "No judgment here. Just, uh, make sure you brush your teeth, OK?"

Iris bared her teeth at him and *grr*ed.

Joe laughed. "Hey, uh, while I've got you . . . Barry *is* still on Earth 38, right? He didn't come back already, did he?"

Iris cocked her head. "No. Why?"

Joe hesitated. She knew the look. She'd beheld that same expression hundreds of times as a kid, when Detective Joe West struggled to answer his daughter's innocent question: "What did you do at work today, Daddy?" The answers often involved too much pain, too much blood, and too much heartache for a child.

"Dad. What's going on? Is it about Barry? Tell me."

Slowly, and with obvious reluctance, Joe told her about his odd encounter on the street with Barry, how the Flash had appeared, battered and bruised, and vanished just as quickly.

For a too-long pause, Iris said nothing, simply worried at her lower lip. Joe allowed her a moment to process it, then said, "Iris? Honey? What's wrong?"

"I . . . I had a similar experience, Dad. I thought it was a dream." And she told him about the day of Anti-Matter Man's breach, how she'd lain down for a quick nap and awoken to a war-torn Barry before her, proclaiming his love before disappearing into thin air.

"What's going on here?" Joe asked.

"I don't know. But I think I know who to ask."

• • •

Caitlin gave Madame Xanadu a clean bill of health. Or at least clean enough to walk down the hall to the room where Iris had had her vision of Barry. The seer wore a hospital gown and walked leaning partly on Iris, partly on a wheeled IV pole that had a bag feeding her a steady drip of fluids.

After too many minutes and too many halting steps, Iris and Madame Xanadu arrived at the room where Iris had napped. After glancing around the room for a few seconds, Madame Xanadu gestured toward the bed. Iris helped her sit there.

"Do you see anything?" Iris asked. "Sense anything?"

"Only your agitation and worry," Madame Xanadu said somewhat wryly.

"He was standing right here." Iris shook off Madame Xanadu's asperity. She needed the woman's help. Positioning herself where she remembered Barry standing, she faced the bed. "I was right where you are."

Madame Xanadu shook her head. "It may have been your imagination."

"My father saw it, too."

"That does not mean it couldn't have been your imagination." Less acerbic now. More gentle. "Iris, if I had access to my draughts and cards, my candles and sachets . . ."

"We can get you whatever you need," Iris said quickly. "This is S.T.A.R. Labs. We do ten crazy things before breakfast. And then after breakfast we really get started."

"I was going to say . . . If I had those things, even then I might not be able to see anything. I feel nothing in this room.

If you had seen a spirit or phantasm, there would be *something* lingering. Psychic residue, if you will."

A spirit. So, a ghost, then. In other words . . . if Barry was already dead.

No. She wouldn't go there. Not even for a second.

"But you *don't* sense any psychic residue."

"Be glad. There is no intimation of death here."

Clinging to the good news, Iris asked, "And you're sure?"

Madame Xanadu shrugged. "My senses are weak. Before, the fifty-two of us amplified each other, lending strength. With one of us gone . . . it's difficult. There's a piece missing, you understand?"

"Like . . . losing a tooth and figuring out which side to chew on now."

Madame Xanadu's lips turned down into an expression of indecision. "I suppose."

With a supreme and—she hoped—invisible effort, Iris tamped down her irritation and disappointment. "I see. Well, thank you for trying."

As she helped the mystic to her feet, Iris asked, "About those teammates who are lost in time . . . I've been wondering—if we brought you something they owned, something they touched . . ."

"I am not a bloodhound, Iris. You cannot simply ask me to pick up a scent and follow it through time."

Iris suppressed an exasperated sigh and steadied Madame Xanadu as the two of them made their way back to the medical bay.

• • •

As Iris and Madame Xanadu turned a corner, a figure emerged from the shadows of a close-by corner.

Owlman watched them go.

So . . . the Flash was not on this Earth. And other members of his team were missing as well. Soon, the twin blankets of desperation and fear would settle over the survivors . . . and begin to smother.

It was almost time to enact his plan.

27

BY THE TIME KARA, J'ONN, AND Barry returned to Superman's hidden workshop under the Kent Farm, Oliver and Kal had come back as well. Brainy, working two computers at once and speaking to himself in three different languages, broke free from his labors as soon as Kara entered and stood silent for a full second as a single tear wended its way down his cheek. Kara knew that to disconnect and focus all twelve of his multitasking threads on one thing was a high compliment.

"Get ahold of yourself, Brainy," she joked.

He wiped the tear away. "I am . . . gratified that you're still alive."

"*Still?*" Superman's tone demanded an immediate answer.

"Brainy says history says I die today," Kara said with as much lightness in her voice as she could muster. "But, you know, history also says that Watson and Crick discovered the structure of DNA, but they wouldn't have gotten anywhere without the work of Rosalind Franklin."

"Yeah," Barry chimed in, reluctantly handing Brainy's flight ring back to him; "and people also think that Alexander Graham Bell invented the telephone and that Columbus discovered America. Sometimes false information perpetuates down through the ages."

"Historical fact or not, we'll need to talk more about Brainy's recollections soon," Superman said in a very no-nonsense tone. "But first . . . Any updates?"

They brought in the DEO on speakerphone, conferencing in Lena and Alex, who both admitted—in voices that betrayed utter exhaustion—that they had nothing new to report. The red skies were spreading, all weapons were useless against Anti-Matter Man, and pretty soon they would need to evacuate more and more cities . . .

"And eventually there will be nowhere to evacuate *to*," Alex finished.

The gang in the workshop shared a silent look of resignation.

"OK, then," Superman said. "Brainiac 5?"

Brainy's only outward sign of nervousness or regret was the way he twisted his Legion flight ring as he spoke. "I have made what could charitably be described as *negligible progress* on the issue of Anti-Matter Man. With thirty-first-century technology and six or seven hours, I could solve our problem. We lack both."

"So when you say *negligible progress* . . ." Barry hinted.

"I mean none."

"This is going well," Oliver said. "Does anyone have any good news?"

"J'Onn tapped into Anti-Matter Man's mind," Kara volunteered.

"You could have led with that announcement," Alex said on speakerphone.

Kara stood behind J'Onn, who sat in a chair, elbows on his knees, haggard and beat. "I wasn't sure if he wanted to talk about it. If he was ready."

"I don't think we have the option of respite," Barry said, not unkindly. He felt more than a little bit woozy after his maiden flight. Maybe his first time flying independently shouldn't have been in circles a few million times.

"If you know something, you need to tell us," Oliver added. "Preferably right now. Otherwise, there won't be a later."

J'Onn nodded his heavy-browed head, not looking up as he spoke. "I used my telepathy to force my way into Anti-Matter Man's mind. *Force* might be the wrong word. I . . . I expected a door. Defenses. But there were none. I barged right in."

"He had no mental defenses?" Barry asked.

"No one thought he would need them," J'Onn said. "He's genetically modified. Artificially conceived and customized. No independent thought or individuality. But he has *memories*, and those I was able to access. To . . . relive." He winced with deep memory. Kara's hand on his arm was a balm against the psychic pain. He nodded to her in gratitude and then told them everything he'd experienced—Anti-Matter Man's "birth" in a gestational chamber, his modification, his imprisonment in the heart of a moon.

"And then someone . . . some*thing* reached back and released him," J'Onn went. "Just . . . cracked open the moon and let him out. Set him on his path."

"Reached *back*?" Barry asked. "What does that mean? Reached back from where?"

"Not where, Flash. When." J'Onn finally looked up, his glowing eyes dimmer than usual and haunted. "I saw through the veil of Time itself, into the future."

Barry stiffened. He thought of Abra Kadabra, the techno-magician from the sixty-fourth century who had so harried him, who had almost conquered the twenty-first century. "How far into the future?" he asked.

J'Onn shuddered with the memory and his voice was hollow when he spoke:

"All the way, Flash. All the way to the end of Time itself."

No one said a word. The room was silent save for the slight hiss of the speakerphone.

"So . . ." Oliver broke the eerie quiet. "Something reached back in time from the end of the universe and broke open a moon to let this living weapon march across the Multiverse. Do I have it right?"

J'Onn nodded mordantly.

Oliver threw his hands in the air. "I don't even know where to go with this."

"Who has that sort of power?" Supergirl asked rhetorically. "Breaking open a moon . . . That's a big ask, even for Kal and me."

"All I know," J'Onn said, his voice gathering some heat and strength, "is that whoever or whatever it was, the enemy from the future used a special machine to open the breaches through the Multiverse for Anti-Matter Man. A machine powered by a person. I caught a glimpse of a man within that machine, running in a circle. Moving fast. Like you do, Flash. Only, he was a yellow blur."

Barry froze in place. Oliver whispered, "Damn it."

A yellow blur. A man in yellow.

Eobard Thawne. The Reverse-Flash. The man who'd killed Barry's mother, the man who'd killed Ronnie Raymond. The man who had almost destroyed the world as part of his mad, narcissistic quest to heap misery upon the Flash.

"This makes a little more sense," Barry said to them all. "If the Reverse-Flash is involved . . . that explains the time travel aspect of things. He's teamed up with others before. At least we know he's at the heart of this."

"How does that help?" Oliver spluttered. "We're still facing an extinction-level event on Earth 38 in the next hour or so—"

"Forty-nine minutes and seventeen seconds," Brainy interrupted.

"—and we have no way to get to the end of Time to punch your old nemesis in the face *and* I can't believe I just said that sentence out loud!"

"We have to do *something*," Kara put in. "It's getting worse and worse out there. The damage is contained right now, but according to Brainy and Lena's calculations, in forty-nine minutes—"

"Forty-eight minutes and thirty-two seconds."

"—we'll cross the threshold, the point of no return. We can't let that happen! Now is the time for your craziest ideas! Anyone?"

Superman folded his arms over his chest and gazed around the room. "Kara's right. If you've been holding back because you think your idea is silly or unworkable, speak up now. Please."

Barry shook his head. He had nothing. Neither did Oliver.

J'Onn looked at the floor again.

"All my ideas require a functioning Miracle Machine," said Brainiac 5. "And Matter-Eater Lad ate . . . *will eat* . . . the last one in existence."

No one spoke.

And then, over the speakerphone, Alex:

"If you ask me, you all are thinking too hard. Sometimes, you have to throw fancy strategies and tactics out the window and just *hit* something."

Kara's and Barry's eyes met. He shrugged.

She looked over at Superman, who stared briefly, then smiled confidently.

"She's not wrong, you know. And I'm up to something like ninety-nine point five percent."

Kara nodded resolutely and punched her fist into her palm. "That'll have to do. Let's go."

Supergirl, Superman, and the Martian Manhunter rose into the red sky, leaving Oliver, Brainy, and Barry behind. The red skies had spread to surrounding communities now. It was too late to evacuate anyone, but the three of them could work to contain the damage and keep people safe.

Brainiac 5 took to the skies at a lower altitude, pinpointing trouble spots for the ground team: Barry raced people into shelters while Oliver worked to keep people calm.

The whole time they were saving lives, they wondered, *Is there any point? Is everyone going to die anyway?*

The answer was up in the sky.

28

THE MAN WHO HAD SO STARTLED Cisco and Curtis introduced himself as Ohiyesa Smith. "But you can call me Sheriff," he added.

"Nice to, uh, meet you, Sheriff," Curtis said.

Ohiyesa shrugged. "You know what? You can call me Ohiyesa. Didn't mean to frighten you like that before," he added with a considerate nod to Cisco.

They were sitting around a fire that Ohiyesa had built for them in astonishingly short order. Cisco sometimes had trouble lighting a match, but Ohiyesa slapped together a nice, roaring fire in no time flat. Benefits of living in a pre-electric world, Cisco supposed. Once the sun had set, a chill had settled in pretty quickly. Cisco and Curtis were grateful for the fire.

And even more grateful for the hardtack that Ohiyesa shared out of a pack he'd retrieved from the bushes.

"I wasn't *that* scared," Cisco said defensively.

"You made toddlers look brave," Curtis said. "My arms are still sore from where you dug your nails into them in total fear."

"You were shaking, too!" Cisco shouted. "I could feel it!"

"Is everyone from the future so *loud*?" Ohiyesa asked, wincing.

"Sorry," Cisco said. "Look, we've been meaning to ask . . ."

"What makes you think we're from the future?" Curtis finished.

Ohiyesa took a bite of biscuit and stared at them across and through the flickering flames as he chewed. "Well, it helps that when I suggested it, you didn't look at me like I ought to be locked up in a padded room somewhere. And I overheard a little of your yapping when I sneaked up on you. But mostly it was your clothes."

Cisco and Curtis looked down at themselves and then at each other. Artificial polyleather superhero gear from head to toe. There would be nothing like it in the world for more than a century.

"I've met people from the future before," Ohiyesa said, much to their surprise. "You all from 2024, too?"

Cisco and Curtis glanced at each other: 2024. That was the date on the future newspaper in the hidden Time Vault at S.T.A.R. Labs. The newspaper that declaimed that Barry would disappear.

"We're a little earlier than that."

Ohiyesa nodded slowly and poked at some logs with the toe of his boot, stoking the fire. "Fellas I met were from 2024. Claimed there was some kind of crisis."

Crisis. That had been the word in the newspaper headline.

"We're sort of in the midst of our own crisis right now," Curtis said. "We're stuck here and need to get back."

Ohiyesa frowned. "I'd love to help, but I think that's a bit beyond what we're capable of in the here and now. Plus, I've got an outlaw on the lam I'm trying to track down."

Cisco giggled. *"On the lam.* He actually said it, Curtis. Wow!"

"Can we please focus?" Curtis stared Cisco down. "We know you don't have a time machine, Ohiyesa, but there might be a way for us to contact our friends in the future. Can you tell us where the nearest town is?"

"Elkhorn—that's my town—is about a day's hard ride that way." He pointed to the west. "But you fellas have no horses, so it's more like a week."

Elkhorn. Cisco had never heard of it. Would it still be around in the twenty-first century? And even if so, was there a place where he could stash a note of some sort that would last 150 years? And then how to make sure the note got from Elkhorn to Central City . . .

His head spun.

"You fellas think on it," Ohiyesa said, rising. "I gotta see a man about a horse."

With that, Ohiyesa stepped into the darkness of the copse of trees. "Score! He's gonna get us horses," Cisco whispered to Curtis. "That's a good thing, right?"

Curtis rolled his eyes. "That's not what *seeing a man about a horse* means. It's a way of saying he's going to pee."

"Well, that just . . . That just . . ." Cisco's tone was offended. "That just makes no sense!"

"Right. And *that* is the problem here, not how to get home."

Duly chastened, Cisco shivered, then rubbed his hands together and held them out to the fire.

"What if we bury something?" Curtis said out of nowhere. "A message to the others."

"There's more than a century between now and when we need to be. Do you have any idea how many times this land will be dug up, bulldozed, shifted around between now and then?"

"No," Curtis admitted. "And neither do you. For all you know, it could be perfectly safe."

"And it could also fail miserably. Are we going to salt the earth with notes to the future? What happens if the wrong people dig them up?"

"We could breach somewhere with banks, safety-deposit boxes . . ." Curtis surmised. "What about New York City? It's a place in this time period and you know it, so you could get us there, right?"

Cisco pondered this. "Yeah, but the layout of the city isn't the same. I could breach us right into a wall."

"OK, so how about some place you know better? What's Central City like in this time period?"

Cisco shrugged. "Confession time: During history class in high school, I used to hide behind my textbook and read comic books and Stephen Hawking. To me, history is, like, the invention of break dancing and then a big blur of everything that happened before that."

"That's just sad."

"Oh?" Cisco snorted. "How about you, Mr. Seventeen Doctorates? Where's your history degree?"

Curtis opened his mouth to say something, then thought better of it as the rustle of bushes presaged Ohiyesa's return. With a start, he slapped at Cisco's shoulder.

"Ow! Hey!" Cisco pushed back, shoving Curtis.

Raising his eyebrows significantly, Curtis jerked his head toward Ohiyesa. Cisco finally looked up and directed his attention there.

Ohiyesa stood with a sheepish look on his face, both arms raised high above his head. Behind him and off to one side stood a small woman with red hair, the lower half of her face concealed by a white bandanna. She wore a close-fitting white top and pants, along with a yellow gun belt. Both holsters were empty.

Because one of the guns was held on Ohiyesa, the barrel touching the side of his neck.

And the other was aimed right at Cisco.

"Oh, hi there," Cisco said, swallowing nervously at the sight of the very large revolver aimed at his head. "You must be on the lam."

29

"ENTER FREELY," THE WOMAN NAMED Madame Xanadu said, "and unafraid."

Sneering from his position in the doorway to her room, Owlman crossed his arms over his chest. "I'm not afraid. And I'll enter when I please, not a moment before. But don't even think about hitting your nurse button to summon them."

Owlman was accustomed to the threat in his voice eliciting shivers and quakes in his prey. But Madame Xanadu merely sat up straighter in her hospital bed and clucked her tongue in impatience.

"I have no desire to summon them, Bruce. I've been waiting for you. So that we can talk."

"Waiting for me?" For a moment, Owlman experienced an emotion that he could not identify, something unfamiliar and foreign.

Then he realized: It was fear. It had been so long since he'd felt it that he didn't recognize it at first.

Fools blustered and bludgeoned their way through fear. The wise man knew to harness it and hold back.

"Why have you been waiting?" he asked her.

Madame Xanadu crossed her fingers before her, then suddenly jerked them apart. In the space between her hands there somehow appeared a wash of colors and shades that quickly resolved into spinning orbs. Owlman picked out what looked like the Earth among a field of stars . . . but then another Earth . . .

And another . . .

And another . . .

"I've been lying to Iris West-Allen and her friends," Madame Xanadu revealed, her face lit by the glow of the universes she'd conjured. "All so that I could meet you, Bruce Wayne. I know what is to come. It is time for you to encounter your destiny. It's time for you to understand . . . *everything*."

30

JOE, DIG, AND DINAH PORED OVER data purloined from Star City hotels and home shares, looking for anything that might lead them to Ambush Bug. They weren't foolish enough to hope that he'd registered under his actual name, but, as Joe said, "I've seen criminals do stupider things."

There were more than eight hundred hotels in Star City, more than two hundred of which met their criteria for "swanky." And then there were something like four *thousand* home rentals in the right price range for someone looking to impress the sort of rich blackguards who would buy some deadly, stolen robot bees.

Deadly, stolen robot bees. Joe still couldn't believe this was the world he lived in.

His eyes were bloodshot as he continued skimming the rental and hotel listings. Exactly what they hoped to find, none of them knew for certain. They just studied each listing, hoping that *something* would jump out at them as being related to Irwin Schwab.

"What about this one?" Dinah held out her tablet to the other two. "Zenobia Irwin. Booked two nights at the Star City Plaza Hotel."

"Could be," Joe said.

"Put it on the list," Dig said.

She added the name to a meager list they'd cobbled together thus far. Wild Dog was in the field, working his way down the hotels as they sent him updates.

"Hello, hello!" said a familiar voice.

Everyone looked up to see Felicity Smoak looming over them on the big screen. "I love seeing my worker bees hard at it!" she said. "Pun absolutely intended, BTW. That's my thing now."

"Felicity. Do you have something for us?" Dig's voice, polite and restrained, echoed deeply in the cavernous space of the Bunker.

"Oh! Right!" She grinned. "I do. I put together an algorithm to crunch through every rental application, hotel reservation, and house share in Star City. It kicked back a lot, but one really stood out."

"Give it to us." Joe grabbed a pen and paper.

"You're gonna love it." Her grin widened.

"Just give it to us." Hard and tight, Dinah's tone left no room for further levity. She was ready for this nonsense to end.

"Fine, fine." Deep breath, and then Felicity said, "One week ago, someone reserved a large suite at the Grand Starling Hotel on Kirby Street for three nights, beginning last night. The name on the reservation is . . . Are you ready for it?"

"Felicity!" All three of them yelled it.

"Wow, OK! Gee, can't a girl enjoy the drama a little? The name on the reservation is Alphonse Michael Bush."

They all got it in about two seconds, but Joe got there first. "A. M. Bush," he said. "Unbelievable."

"He made that reservation *before* the bees made him go crazy?" Dig asked. "Was this guy *ever* sane?"

"Like I said before: Criminals do stupid things."

Dinah nodded a curt thanks at Felicity and stood. "Ping Wild Dog. Let's move."

The lobby of the Grand Starling Hotel redefined the word *opulent*. It stretched up three floors, the second and third ringed by balconies with clear glass balustrades and polished brass railings. Massive windows gave sunlight ingress from 360 degrees, and a truly enormous crystal chandelier hung from the distant ceiling, its teardrop stones glimmering in the light like stars dragged down from the heavens. Sumptuous couches and easy chairs upholstered in buttery, satiny brown leather completed the look, arranged around a fire roaring within a white marble fireplace that towered overhead and disappeared somewhere around the third floor.

Dressed in his civvies—black jeans and a dark gray hoodie that had seen better days—Rene Ramirez sauntered over to the others as they entered.

"Glad you all got here. Another minute and I think the manager was gonna throw me out for stinking up his classy joint." He jerked his chin in the direction of an officious and offended-looking man in his late forties who wore a pristine black suit and tie. The man was fidgeting with a cell phone, turning it over and over in his hands.

"You're up, Dinah," Joe said. "It's your town."

Dinah hitched up her gun belt and strode over to the manager. As the three men watched, she flashed her Star City Police Department badge and ID. The manager did a double take and nodded hurriedly before dashing behind the registration desk. He returned in a moment, slipped something to Dinah, and then hustled off, the cell phone held to his ear.

Dinah strolled over to the guys, waving a key card. "I have the key to his room. Let's go ambush Ambush."

Dig and Joe stood on either side of the door to what they hoped would turn out to be Ambush Bug's suite, their weapons drawn. Rene stood across the hall, his gun out and aimed at the door. Dinah leaned past Joe and waved the key card at the door. The lock clicked open.

Joe reached over with his free hand and *slo-o-o-o-o-wly* turned the doorknob, then pushed the door open. Nice hotel: The hinges didn't squeak a peep.

Dig rolled his back along the doorjamb, gliding into the room with much more speed and grace than his big frame would imply. Rene followed, followed by Dinah, with Joe slipping in last and silently shutting the door.

Don't know why I bothered. You do that so the perp can't just run out the door, but this guy can teleport. Old habits die hard.

They fanned out. The suite was huge. They'd entered into a living room, which had a large picture window looking out onto the Star City skyline. Pristine white leather sofa. Two easy chairs. A glass coffee table edged in gold that Joe figured would cost at least a month's pay. Before taxes.

He signaled to the others. There were four doors, all of them closed. They each took one.

Joe's opened into a bathroom, as sumptuously appointed as the rest of the suite. Its occupant, though, had not been kind to it. Wet towels were heaped on the marble floor. A roll of toilet paper lay on the vanity, half unrolled down to the floor. A crushed tube of toothpaste bled sparkly green gel into the sink. Puddles of water lay on every surface, and the shower—which was bigger than the bedroom in Joe's first apartment—drip-drip-dripped water from its waterfall showerhead.

Satisfied that there was nothing in here for him, Joe backed out, weapon still drawn. Dig was just emerging from his door, shaking his head. Nothing in there.

Rene leaned in his door and shrugged noncommittally.

That left Dinah. The three men converged in the middle of the living room. Just as they began making their way to Dinah's door, her hand appeared there, gesturing them in.

They gathered there. Dinah stood just inside what they now saw was a bedroom. *Bedroom* might have been too small a word for it—if the bathroom here was bigger than Joe's first bedroom, the bedroom was bigger than his first studio apartment altogether. In the center of it was an enormous California king bed that seemed to float in midair. The headboard rose to the ceiling. Curtains were drawn tightly across the windows, and an open door revealed a second bathroom.

Lying in the middle of the bed, curled in a ball, was Ambush Bug.

"He's still wearing the suit?" Rene hissed.

Joe shot him a fierce *Shut up!* look. They didn't want to wake the guy before they could get to him. Feeling at his belt, Joe located the Cisco Ramon–created S.T.A.R. Labs meta-dampening handcuffs. He hoped they would work on Ambush Bug's weird combination of tech. If not, this would be the shortest arrest in history.

With a series of gestures, Joe indicated to everyone what he wanted them to do: Dig on one side of the bed, Rene at the foot, Dinah hanging back, ready to use her Canary Cry, if necessary. Joe himself would come up on the final side of the bed, behind Ambush Bug, and slap the cuffs on him.

Hopefully, it would work.

They settled into position. Joe realized he would need to lean on the bed in order to reach Ambush Bug's wrists. Would doing that jostle him? Wake him?

Something else was bothering Joe, too. Something was off about all of this. Something was missing. It nagged at him. It . . .

It *bugged* him.

Across the bed, on the other side of Ambush Bug, Dig spread his arms wide with a *What are you waiting for, man?* expression on his face. Rene looked just as put out.

The bees, Joe mouthed.

After a second, it hit all of them: Where were Ambush Bug's robot bees? Even with the dim light in the room, they should have been able to see *some* of them.

Shaking his head to dislodge the sudden worry, Joe silently slid his weapon into its holster and transferred the meta-dampening cuffs to his right hand.

That was when he heard the buzzing.

They *all* heard it. All four of them turned to look at the bathroom door, slightly ajar. Shadows flitted in there. Moving.

"Do it!" Dig whispered harshly.

Joe figured he had no choice; leaning forward, he planted one knee on the bed. Some part of him thought, *Wow, this is really comfortable!* But the rest of him could only focus on those green-sleeved wrists just before him.

The buzzing intensified. Joe moved forward farther, putting his other knee on the bed, and the cuffs slid onto Ambush Bug's left wrist—

Pop!

The Bug was gone.

Pop!

"Behind you!" Dig yelled. Joe threw himself forward, flat on the bed, as Diggle fired his weapon.

Zing! Zing! Bullets zipped over Joe's head.

Pop! Pop!

"Get him!" Dig yelled. "Get him!"

"Stand back!" Dinah shouted.

Joe rolled over. There were bullet holes in the wall near the bathroom door, a swarm of bees purling forth from where the door was open, but no Ambush Bug.

"Hey!" said a familiar voice. "Who's that sleeping in my bed, Papa Bear?"

Joe shrieked and jumped up. Ambush Bug was right next to him!

"None of you look like Goldilocks!" the Bug shouted. "You're doing it all wrong!"

Pop! He appeared up near the ceiling.

"No guns!" Joe cried. "Dinah!"

Dinah licked her lips and opened her mouth—

—pop!—

—and Ambush Bug appeared in front of her, shoving a hotel washcloth in her mouth. "Cleanliness is next to the Burger King on Fourth Avenue," he said. "Mom always said that. Gosh, I miss her."

He *pop!*ed away and they all stared at one another for a moment. Belatedly, Dinah pulled the washcloth out of her mouth.

"How did—"

Pop! He was back, this time right behind Rene, whom he grabbed with an arm around the throat, immobilizing his gun with his other hand.

"Shoot . . . him . . . !" Rene gasped.

"Tsk, tsk!" said the Bug. "You shouldn't play with guns. Someone could get hurt. Maybe when you're older and more mature."

"Says the guy who sleeps in his whacked-out super-villain costume!" Dig taunted, trying to get a clear shot.

"Costume?" Ambush Bug frowned. The mask had gotten a little tighter on him—his facial expressions were visible through it. "This isn't a costume, man. It's my *skin*. It ain't easy being green, you know. Just ask J'Onn J'Onzz. Or that Brainiac 5 kid. Although he's really more a bluish color in this particular version, isn't he? And even then, only when it's in the budget that week."

He wrestled Rene's gun from his hand, then—

—*pop! pop!*—

—appeared at Joe's side to grab *his* gun and then—

—*pop! pop!*—

—materialized at Dig's side, swiping *his* gun—

—*pop! pop!*—

—and appeared next to Dinah. Who was ready for him. She'd drawn in a breath at his penultimate *pop!* and as soon as she saw Ambush Bug again, she screamed her Canary Cry.

Dig, Joe, and Rene clapped their hands over their ears, but they needn't have worried—Dinah had focused her Cry right on Ambush Bug, and they weren't in the cone of danger emanating forth from between her lips. But Ambush Bug was. The Cry swallowed his screech of agony, but his expression revealed all his pain. So powerful was the Cry that it actually lifted him bodily and tossed him across the room.

Dig dodged at the last second and Ambush Bug hurtled past him, colliding with the padded headboard and then crashing onto the bed.

He lay still as Dinah cut off the Canary Cry. The room suddenly seemed too loudly quiet.

"Is he dead?" Joe asked.

"Hope so," Rene said, massaging his throat.

Dinah shook her head. "I doubt it. I didn't hit him *that* hard."

As though he had something to prove, Ambush Bug shakily sat up, twisting his neck this way and that. "Oh, wow," he said, slouched against the headboard. "That was like acupuncture plus a lobotomy at the same time." He tapped his skull with one finger.

"I feel better than ever! My head is so clear! Everything is so obvious!"

"Great," Joe muttered. Their weapons were all on the bed, lying on the pillows around Ambush Bug. No way to get them without alerting him. He signaled to Dinah that she might need to zap the guy again.

"You know, gang, I gotta tell you—I know it was just to fulfill a plot point, but being stung almost to death by a swarm of bees is the best thing that ever happened to me! And I'm so happy about it that I want to share the wealth!"

"I don't think I like the sound of that," Dig warned. Dinah drew in a threatening breath.

"Everyone should have the powers I have!" Ambush Bug chortled. "Everyone should see the world the way I do! I'm gonna let loose a swarm of bees on the city, to deliver the good news in a million beestings!"

Pop!

He was gone from the room before anyone could move. Then, as they stood there in shock, the swarm of bees from the bathroom surged and squirted through the opening, soaring past Joe and Dig, headed for the window.

They hit the glass as a mass—any one or two or dozen bees would have splatted against the pane, but with so many of them hitting at once, the glass shattered and the cloud of robot bees exploded out into the Star City night.

"Was he serious?" Rene asked. "Is he gonna set those things loose on the whole city?"

"He's *never* serious," Dig said. "His whole gig is that he's never serious."

"I don't know," Joe said, crawling onto the bed to retrieve his service weapon. "He sounded different at the end there. I think Dinah's yell might have shaken something loose."

"Or shaken something back into place," Dinah supplied.

"Yeah." Joe ran a hand through his hair. "This is officially out of our bailiwick. Probably has been for a while. We need to call in some serious backup."

31

THE THREE OF THEM CONVERGED on Anti-Matter Man more than twenty thousand feet straight up. Up here, the air was frigid and thin. It reminded J'Onn of Mars.

Anti-Matter Man stood more than three hundred feet tall, walking calmly toward them as though there was solid ground beneath his feet, not a vast welter of empty space. His expression did not change in the slightest—he was impassive, implacable, resolute. The air around him crackled with constant mini-explosions and eruptions on the atomic level, filling the space nearby with the reek of ozone and burning carbon.

Soon, they would test whether or not Kryptonian and Martian invulnerability could resist the explosive result of matter meeting anti-matter.

"I'll try first," Superman said. "I've tussled with him before."

"Remember what happened?" Kara asked, a little more tartly than she'd intended.

If he was offended, Superman didn't show it. "Still looking out for me? I promise I'll be careful. Watch what I do and what he does, then use that information for your attack run."

Before Kara could speak, he sped away, fists extended before him, plunging toward Anti-Matter Man. With a skipped heart-beat, she realized the import of what he'd just said: He intended his assault as a dry run for her and J'Onn.

He planned to sacrifice himself so that they could see how Anti-Matter Man fought and defended himself and look for a weakness.

"No!" she cried, and would have followed him in an instant had J'Onn not restrained her with a bear hug from behind.

"Kara! This is the end of the world, and your cousin is willing to die to prevent that. Honor his decision!"

"No!" she shouted again, struggling against J'Onn. "The world needs him!"

"The world needs to survive," he reminded her. "Watch and learn."

He was right. In that moment, Kara hated him for it, but J'Onn was right. She relaxed into him, stopped fighting. Together, they observed as Superman arced in the air toward Anti-Matter Man. Bolts of black lightning spat-crackled around the Man of Steel—he dodged them effortlessly, zigging and zagging through the red sky.

J'Onn's bear hug became an embrace. She wrapped her arms around his lower arms, and they held each other like that, watching.

Superman pulled to a hovering stop thirty yards away from

Anti-Matter Man. He drifted there for a moment and then blasted out with his heat vision.

"Good move," Kara muttered. "Not touching him direct—"

She was cut off at the sight of Anti-Matter Man moving with incredible speed for something so large. At the same time, he grew even more. Superman *had* been safely out of the creature's reach, but now Anti-Matter Man extended his arm and brutally backhanded Superman, swatting him with a sizzle-*thwack* that J'Onn and Kara could have heard at their distance even without super-senses. As Kara watched, horrified, Superman tumbled through the air, gathering speed as he went, careening over the horizon. A glance with her telescopic vision told her that he'd already shot over the Pacific and was on a collision course with the Himalayan mountain range.

And something inside Kara Zor-El broke in that moment.

She'd been sent to Earth with one mission, one task: To protect her baby cousin, Kal-El. A glitch in the plan had seen her in suspended animation in the Phantom Zone for years, and by the time she'd arrived on Earth, baby Kal-El was already a grown man, renowned the world over as a hero.

But still—she was supposed to protect him, and now she'd just watched as that beast from the antiverse slapped him like a gnat. Her *cousin. Superman.*

"No. Freaking. *Way,*" she growled.

J'Onn had already slackened his grip on her. It was easy enough to slip out of his grasp. She poured on the speed, flying straight toward Anti-Matter Man.

"Kara!" J'Onn yelled, and flew after her.

"No one hurts my family while I'm around! And you *especially* don't get to hurt Superman!" She didn't know if she was talking to J'Onn or to Anti-Matter Man. It didn't matter. She wasn't going to stand by as Superman rose from his deathbed, only to be smacked down again. Nope.

Anti-Matter Man sensed her coming. Maybe it was the perturbation of the winds caused by her flight. Maybe it was just his ability. She didn't know. He turned toward her, focusing those enormous eyes in her direction. His expression did not change at all. It was impassive and emotionless. Remorseless.

If you're just a thing, I will break you, she thought. *And if you're alive . . . I'll kill you.*

32

NOW, LOOK, THERE'S NO NEED TO do anything foolish," Ohiyesa said, his voice rock-steady and very calm.

Cisco had the impression that this wasn't the first time the sheriff had had a gun pointed at his head.

For that matter, it wasn't the first time *Cisco* had had a gun aimed at him. But he couldn't find it in him to be so unperturbed. It was a *gun*.

"I'm not in the habit of doing foolish things, Sheriff." The woman's voice betrayed no nervousness or agitation. She might have been asking him to pass the salt at dinner. Did they pass the salt in the Old West? Cisco wondered, then snapped himself out of it.

She went on: "But I'm also not in the habit of letting the long arm of the law dictate to me. I can't let you stop me from getting back to Mesa City."

"And I can't let you get there," Ohiyesa said mildly. "You

stole from the Clanton family back in Elkhorn. If I let you get away with that, they're gonna take away my star. And then I go back to being called 'Pow-Wow' Smith."

"That seems kinda racist," Curtis commented.

"The past is *not* a good time to be a person of color in this country," Cisco added.

Curtis snorted. "Wake me up when it is."

Cisco pondered that for about half a second. "Good point."

Ohiyesa shrugged with a casualness that belied his situation. "White people," he said with a *What are you gonna do?* tone in his voice.

"White people," Cisco and Curtis agreed in sync.

"Hey!" the woman shouted.

"No offense!" Cisco said hurriedly. She did still have a gun trained on him, after all.

"I'm not talking about that!" she exclaimed. "But in case you haven't noticed, I'm the one with the guns. Typical men—not taking a woman seriously even though she's in the position of power."

"Man, when did the Wild West become so woke?" Cisco asked.

"I'm going to need your horse, Sheriff," the woman went on, ignoring him. "Seeing's how you were inconsiderate enough to shoot mine out from under me. And then I'll tie you all up. But don't worry—I'll let the folks in Mesa know you're here."

"That's mighty kind of you," Ohiyesa said, "but by the time you get there and let them know, we'll be dead."

"Maybe," she said, and shrugged.

"I've never known Madame .44 to kill a lawman," Ohiyesa said.

Madame .44? Cisco couldn't suppress a frisson of excitement. That was *such* a Wild West name.

"You're not giving me much of a choice," Madame .44 told him, and jabbed the gun at him threateningly. "You should have stayed back in Elkhorn and just let me go on my way."

"Well, like I said—the people of Elkhorn frown on their lawmen letting crooks get away with robbery, grand theft, and the like."

"Your dedication is admirable," Madame .44 admitted. "I hope they put it on your tombstone."

"As long as it doesn't say 'Pow-Wow,'" Ohiyesa said.

While the two of them were talking, Curtis and Cisco had been swapping a series of gestures, eyebrow movements, and flicks of their eyes in certain directions. Cisco was pretty sure he understood the plan and it made sense. It should work.

Then again, the last plan he'd made that should have worked had sent him here. So who knew?

Still, a criminal in any era was a criminal, period. And he was a superhero. So . . .

"Look!" Curtis shouted.

Madame .44's lower face was covered by the bandanna, but Cisco thought he detected a smirk from the way her eyes narrowed and crinkled. "How stupid do you think I am?"

"What in the—?" Ohiyesa gasped.

That made Madame .44 turn just the slightest bit to her left. There, gently pulsating, a breach undulated between her and the copse of trees, its blue light wavering. Cisco's forehead furrowed with the effort of the breach. He couldn't just make a breach without knowing where it led, and this one was headed straight to the Grand Canyon. So great a distance, though, took its toll on him. Sweat began to gather at his hairline. He wasn't sure how long he could maintain this.

"Go," he said to Curtis. "Now."

Mr. Terrific bounced off the balls of his feet, launching himself at Madame .44 while she was distracted. He shouldered her with a perfect body check, knocking her to one side. At the same time, he stiff-armed her right hand, knocking her aim askew to protect Cisco *and* grab the wrist of the other hand, the one pointing a gun at Ohiyesa.

That hand jerked and her finger tightened on the trigger. Curtis braced himself for the report of a gunshot, but nothing happened. Just a dry click. Misfire. They'd gotten lucky.

The plan called for him to knock her into the breach, but just as they toppled toward it, it shrank into a bright pinprick of light and vanished. In the same instant, Cisco cried out in pain and frustration.

"Sorry!" he gasped. "Couldn't maintain it!"

Madame .44 crashed to the ground with Mr. Terrific on top of her. He pinned her down, holding both her arms away from her so that she couldn't aim her guns. Ohiyesa stepped over to them and bent down, prying the weapons from her hands.

"Well, well," said the sheriff, standing over her. "Madame .44, the Outlaw Queen. This looks like the end of your reign, Your Majesty."

33

CHINESE SEISMOLOGISTS IN BEIJING couldn't believe their eyes—according to their instruments, a 2.1 magnitude earthquake had just broken out in the Nepalese mountains. Just as quickly as it had begun, it subsided.

No one knew that what their instruments had detected wasn't actually an earthquake. It was the crash impact of Superman's invulnerable body smashing into Mount Everest at roughly two thousand miles per hour.

The impact crater erupted, a gash measuring nearly as wide as a football field. In the center of it, the Man of Steel did not move as an avalanche, triggered by his collision, dumped more than two tons of snow on him.

Kara had never measured her speed against J'Onn's. She'd always suspected that he was just a tiny bit faster than she was, but she had a head start and the potent fuel of determination. He was yelling at her telepathically, urging her to stop, to retreat, to make a plan with him, but she was beyond listening. And she *had* a plan.

Anti-Matter Man's reaction to Kal's heat vision had been to lash out. Clearly, the heat vision had hurt the creature. Now that she knew how fast it could move and that it could grow beyond its already enormous height, she had the workings of a strategy.

She glided to a stop just outside the creature's reach and fired off her heat vision at Anti-Matter Man's shoulder. Before Anti-Matter Man could react, she shot ten feet to the left and forty feet straight down, then—as Anti-Matter Man lashed out where she'd been a second ago—exhaled a super-cold blast of breath at the same spot where she'd used her heat vision.

What are you doing? J'Onn asked, hovering out of reach.

Alternating extremes of hot and cold, she told him, dodging Anti-Matter Man again and zapping his shoulder with heat vision for the second time.

I see. Rapidly switching between attack methods could confuse his defenses.

Exactly.

Good idea. I'm very proud of you.

Kara couldn't grin because she was puckering up for another run with her super-breath, swinging in a high arc over Anti-Matter Man, her eyes locked on her target—his left shoulder. She inhaled deeply—

Kara! Look out!

What—?

Pain lanced through her body, fire unlike anything she'd ever felt before, and a squeezing, crushing pressure like being buried under a mountain range. She'd been so focused on Anti-Matter Man's left shoulder that she'd neglected to keep an eye on his right arm, and he'd reached out and snagged her out of the sky like a fielder shagging a pop-up. She screamed involuntarily with the sheer agony of it. It was a pain worse even than kryptonite. As though all the fires of Rao had centered on her. She was an exploding sun.

Kara! J'Onn swooped in a circle, building up speed.

No! she thought to him. *Stay . . . back . . . !* Even thinking hurt. She could feel her flesh burning, could smell her hair as the ends of it exploded where it brushed against Anti-Matter Man's thumb.

Brainy had predicted this moment. No, *predicted* was the wrong word. He had *known.* As a little boy on Colu, he'd read in a book (or had had implanted in his memory by a computer) some dry historical fact: *Oh, and then there was the day Anti-Matter Man came to Earth and killed Supergirl. This will not be on the test.*

The pain made her brain do crazy things. She couldn't get the thought of little boy Brainy, wearing shorts and a T-shirt that said I ❤ MOTHERBOARD, out of her mind. A little green-blue alien computer boy, stowing away that factoid for the one time in history it would actually be useful.

And she hadn't listened.

All of a sudden, she experienced a great and powerful peace. Even as her skin began to smolder, a wave of comprehension washed over her.

This was the day.

This was the day she was to die. And she understood that. And she knew, in a blinding moment of clarity, what that meant.

I'm so sorry, Uncle Jor and Aunt Lara: I won't be able to watch over your son anymore.

She wept but shed no tears—they were wicking away and evaporating instantly in the heat of the fires erupting around her.

I'm sorry, Mother. I have to go be with Father now.

Kara? It was J'Onn. Eavesdropping on her thoughts. That was OK. She didn't mind. Someone should know her last words, her last thoughts.

It's going to be OK, J'Onn. I know what to do.

With that, she curled herself into as tight a ball as she could manage within Anti-Matter Man's grasp. She held in her breath for a moment, allowing herself only to *feel*. Transcending the pain, she felt the strength of his massive hand around her body, felt the power coursing through.

Felt the weak points.

Anti-Matter Man was enormous and powerful, true, but he'd been built by his creators on a human framework. That meant that he had relatively weak points, just like a human being would. His fingers, for example, were weaker at the joints.

Kara whispered a prayer to Rao and then thrust out her arms and legs at the same time, aiming for those finger joints. Anti-Matter Man's grip slackened just enough that she spilled free, dropping out of his grasp and zipping out of arm's reach for a moment.

J'Onn was on the other side of Anti-Matter Man. He couldn't get to her in time, not without coming dangerously close to Anti-Matter Man's grasp.

Kara! Gods of Mars . . . ! Get back to the workshop! Let Brainy—

She must have looked pretty bad for J'Onn to swear by the Martian gods.

It's OK, J'Onn. I know what to do.

Her lips set in a grim line, Kara pulled away from Anti-Matter Man, putting some distance between them. The creature's head swiveled toward her, then back to J'Onn, the closer threat.

"Don't even think of hurting him!" she shouted. "I'm not done with you!"

If Anti-Matter Man heard or understood, he gave no indication. He reached out for J'Onn, who nimbly dodged. But just barely.

It was time.

Time for her to do what only she could do. She was the only one left who could stop Anti-Matter Man. Even though it would mean sacrificing . . . everything.

Say goodbye for me, J'Onn.

Although every inch of her body ached and screamed in agonized protest, Kara thrust her fists forward and zoomed toward Anti-Matter Man at top speed.

Alex had been right. Sometimes, you just had to *hit* something.

In the Himalayas, the snow from the avalanche finally settled into place, resting in placid, pure white heaps as though nothing else had ever been there.

Kara sped toward Anti-Matter Man, who was momentarily distracted by J'Onn, who darted and flitted around, shape-shifting into various forms as he did so, baffling the creature's senses.

It felt as though every cell—every *atom*—in her body was combusting. At her speed, it took no more than a second to reach Anti-Matter Man.

But her mind moved faster than her body. She thought of all she would leave behind: Her mother, on Argo. Her adoptive mother, in Midvale. Her sister and her friends . . . James and Lena and J'Onn and everyone else. And Kal, of course, who would have to carry on, who would continue being the world's greatest hero. Because he wasn't capable of anything less.

Wind blew her tears away.

Rao, guide me.

Kara! J'Onn thought to her. *Break off! Get back!*

No! There's one thing we still haven't tried!

What?

She grinned despite what was about to happen. *Everything!*

Anti-Matter Man turned away from J'Onn suddenly, spotting her there, almost atop him. It was too late. For all his power, for all his speed, nothing could stop her now.

With all the strength in her body, with all her considerable velocity behind her, she plowed straight into Anti-Matter Man's chest at ten times the speed of sound.

I love you all, she thought. And then: *Youngest Wheeler-Nicholson winner in history. Not bad.*

Her skin ignited again. The world exploded around her. J'Onn's scream drowned in a welter of eruptions and the sound of Anti-Matter Man's chest caving in. It sounded like concrete in a blender.

It wasn't enough. It wouldn't be enough. He was too powerful.

So she did *everything*.

And unleashed her Super Flare.

J'Onn watched, horrified, as it happened.

He'd been telepathically linked to Kara as she made her suicide run. He knew what she planned to do. And he'd had a split-second image of the Super Flare—bright and yellow-blue—in her mind just before she actually released it.

Super Flare. The ultimate Kryptonian superpower. Kara had expended the totality of her solar-fueled power in a single, mind-numbingly forceful burst of energy. In that instant, she would lose *all* her powers.

Including her invulnerability.

He went blind for a moment, staggered and teetering in the sky. When his vision cleared, he beheld a boiling, flaming hell suspended in the sky: a miasma of noisome, choking clouds and surges of fire bursting out in all directions.

Anti-Matter Man's body had exploded from the inside, his entire structure igniting like fireworks. As his form rapidly dissolved into fire and smoke, J'Onn skipped back a hundred feet or so, beyond the range of the spurts of energy and heat. Anti-Matter Man was no more.

But at what cost? Superman, dead. And Kara . . .

He imagined her, in the middle of that explosion, her powers gone, drained away by the Super Flare . . .

Totally unprotected.

Now he beheld a small figure at the center of the storm.

Kara.

She was falling.

He flew forward. A bolt of black lightning, still crashing across the reddened sky, split the air in his path; he pulled up in barely enough time to avoid being fried by it. The air sizzled and went stale in its wake. J'Onn looked around again. The world was full of smoke, clouded and clotted.

And Kara was nowhere to be seen.

34

BARRY LOOKED UP. SOME DISTANCE behind him and quite a distance up, there'd been a massive *BOOM* that had rattled windows all around him and set off a surfeit of car alarms. He grabbed Oliver, who was nearby, leaning against a mailbox in exhaustion.

"Look!" He pointed to the horizon, above which blossomed a cloud of black smoke and fire.

"I see it," Oliver told him, squinting into the distance. "A blind person could see it. It's like another sun up there. Do you think that's good news or bad news?"

"Good news!" Brainiac 5's voice crackled over the comms channel. "They did it! We read diminishing quantities of anti-matter in the sky!"

"We're confirming via satellite," Lena chimed in from the DEO. "The anti-matter decay effect has halted!"

Cheers went up at the DEO, so loud that Barry and Oliver could hear them over Lena's comms.

"How did they do it?" Barry asked, running to one side to help a young girl and her pet hamster navigate the crowded sidewalk. People were still heading to the local school's tornado shelter, even though he wasn't sure that was necessary any longer.

"No idea." It was Alex this time. "We lost contact with them early on. We're trying to raise them, but there's so much radiation and static in the atmosphere that we can't get a lock—"

"She's falling! She's falling!" J'Onn's scream suddenly broke through on comms. "I can't see through the smoke and the lightning! Someone has to get her!"

Barry froze in the midst of helping the girl. "J'Onn?" He tapped the comms bud in his left ear. "Does anyone read me?"

"Flash, this is Brainiac 5. We have no comms with Supergirl or Superman, but we're reading her tracking beacon. I can give you her coordinates . . . but you can't fly."

Barry ran through the possibilities in the time it took for Brainy to say the word *fly*. "Give me the coordinates. Now."

Without waiting for the precise coordinates—the two seconds it would take Brainy to reveal them would take too long— Barry dashed at top speed toward the cloud on the horizon. He could figure out the precise location later. *Later* being in a couple of seconds.

Brainy read the coordinates to him. Barry silently thanked Cisco Ramon for building a GPS system into his suit's cowl—an overlay slid into his field of vision, showing exactly where he needed to be.

It turned out to be in the heart of Smallville, right at the intersection of Main and Swan Streets. Barry skidded to a halt, the macadam in his path purling smoke, nearly liquefied by the heat of his running.

Straight above him, a speck in the sky was growing larger and larger.

OK, Allen, time for math . . .

He had no idea how much Kara weighed. She looked like she weighed maybe 110, 115. Was Kryptonian cellular structure denser than a human's, though? For all he knew, she could weigh 500 pounds.

Well, there was no way to know. He would have to overcompensate. Assume she weighed four times more than appearances would allow, and hope that that wasn't too low. If she weighed *less* than his surmise, his plan should still work. If she weighed more . . . Ugh.

Kara had been something like twenty thousand feet up. Fortunately, her mass didn't matter in terms of how fast she would fall, only in how much energy she'd release when she hit. Barry didn't intend for her to hit at all.

Twenty thousand feet . . . Figure roughly six thousand meters . . . So, the formula for how long it takes a falling body to hit the ground is $\sqrt{(2h/9.8)}$ . . . Which means she's got a little over thirty seconds.

Barry grinned. That was all the time in the world.

He started running, moving in a wide circle, then a tighter and tighter one. At his incredible speed, the friction of his running was like putting up a circular wall of heat and energy. As he tightened the circle, the air within had nowhere to go but up. A cushion of air rose into the sky as he ran faster and faster, tighter and tighter.

Running around and around in a circle might entertain toddlers, but for Barry, it wasn't just boring—it was also slightly dangerous. If he got dizzy and stumbled, his super-momentum could carry him through buildings, cars, people . . . It could be a serious problem.

He focused on his feet, digging a furrow in the blacktop as he ran. A little island surrounded by a liquid-tar moat formed as he ran faster and faster, whipping up more and more wind, funneling it into the sky. He didn't dare look up—he could lose his footing.

"Five seconds to impact!" Brainy shouted over the comms.

Barry dug in and kept running.

"Four!" Brainy said.

And then . . .

"Four . . . more?"

Barry couldn't spare the breath for a chuckle, but he allowed himself to think, *Heh.*

"Still four seconds . . . Flash, what are you doing?"

He looked straight up. Two stories aboveground, Kara hung limp in midair, buoyed aloft by Barry's whirlwind. Now it was time to start widening the circle again, so that the volume of updraft air would decrease, lowering her gently to the ground.

A few seconds later, she landed in his arms. *Gently* may have been the wrong word—in his haste to get her down quickly, he'd sacrificed some time and she crashed into him with more force than he'd intended, knocking him off his feet. He dropped to his knees, cradling her as he went.

Supergirl's costume was torn and burned. Her cape was a ragged scrap of material dangling from her shoulders. Her skin was dull and gray, her hair singed at the ends.

She wasn't moving. Or breathing.

"No," he said aloud. "I'm not letting this happen."

"Flash?" It was Alex in his ear. "Flash, do you have her?"

"I need . . ." He couldn't tell Alex. Not over comms. That was no way to hear it. "I need a second, OK, guys?"

"What's going on?" Alex insisted. "Flash, I need a sitrep from you *now*."

Barry yanked back his cowl and ripped the DEO comms bud out of his ear. "Kara? Kara, can you hear me? Kara?"

He felt for a pulse in her wrist and at her neck. Nothing.

This could *not* be. He wouldn't allow it. He hadn't come so far, fought so hard, just to see his friend killed in the endgame.

He put his ear to her chest, listening for breath, for a heartbeat.

Still nothing.

She was dead. Supergirl was dead.

Tears clotted his vision. Barry held her close, his forehead to hers. "Oh God. Oh God, Kara, I'm so sorry. I'm so sorry."

"Flash." Not a voice through comms, of course. He'd thrown the bud away.

Barry looked up. Standing over him, the sun at his back, was Superman, one hand outstretched to him.

"Flash, let me have her. There's still time."

"No. No, I'm sorry, Superman, but she's gone. She's not breathing. There's no heartbeat . . ."

Superman hunkered down across from Barry and gently pried the Scarlet Speedster's fingers from Kara's body.

"You have to trust me, Flash. My hearing's better than yours. But I have to get her to the Fortress right away. Only the medical equipment there can save her now. And I didn't punch my way free of an avalanche just to watch my cousin die."

Barry released her and fell back to sit on the road. He watched as Superman tenderly gathered Kara in his arms and then rose into the air, turning into a red-and-blue blur as he soared north.

35

SULLEN, MADAME .44 SAID NOTHING as Ohiyesa slapped a set of particularly brutal-looking handcuffs on her.

"Thanks for your help, you two," Ohiyesa said once he was satisfied that her shackles were locked tight. "I appreciate it. I've only got the one horse, but I can leave you some supplies, and I'll send a posse back once I hit Elkhorn."

Cisco tried not to let his disappointment show. He'd just helped save an actual Western lawman from some hot lead, and his reward was . . . to rough it in the woods with Mr. Terrific some more?

Still, he supposed it was better than nothing.

"You want the law to go a little easier on you?" Ohiyesa asked Madame .44. "Give up your goods. Show me where you stashed that load of cash and silver you stole from the Clantons."

Madame .44 bristled at the word *stole*. "Stole *back*, you mean," she snarled.

"I'm sure." Ohiyesa pulled her to her feet by the chain between her manacles. "Suit yourself."

"Wait!"

They all turned to Curtis, who was crouched down in the tall grass by the tree line. In his outstretched hands, he held both of Madame .44's six-shooters, which had fallen there when they tackled her to the ground.

"Ah, almost forgot them." Ohiyesa reached out for the weapons.

"No, no, look." Curtis flicked open the weapons' chambers. They were Colt Army revolvers, the kind of pistols Cisco had seen in a thousand Westerns as a kid. In real life, they didn't seem fun at all.

The barrel of each weapon flipped out. There were six slots, one for each bullet, and as you pulled the trigger, the barrel would rotate to the next slot. But as Cisco peered closer, he saw that there were only *five* bullets in each pistol's barrel.

He remembered then—Curtis tackling Madame .44. The dry *click!* as her finger had spasmed on the trigger.

"She left a chamber empty in each gun," Cisco said.

"Yeah. The chamber that was primed," said Mr. Terrific. "So that she *couldn't* shoot us, not even by mistake."

As Curtis pulled himself up to his full height, he and Cisco both turned to stare at Ohiyesa.

"Pretty strange behavior for an 'outlaw queen,' wouldn't you say?" Cisco asked.

With a bemused frown, Ohiyesa gazed at the pistols, then back to Madame .44, who sat silent, not looking at any of them.

Then, with no warning, Ohiyesa snatched away the bandanna around Madame .44's lower face. Her lips were pressed into a tight line, as though resisting something.

"What are you about, lady?" Ohiyesa shook the fist that was crumpling her bandanna. "What kind of plan are you—"

"She didn't want to risk hurting us," Cisco jumped in. "There's more here than meets the eye, Sheriff."

"You said *stole back* before," Curtis reminded her. "What did you mean?"

Madame .44 opened her mouth to speak, then thought better of it and shook her head, remaining silent.

With a snort of disgust, Ohiyesa threw down her bandanna. "You want to stay quiet? You want me to run you back to Elkhorn without a chance to speak your piece?"

Cisco didn't blame her for not speaking. She was a woman, bound and helpless while three men stood over her. He sat down on the grass next to her, tucking his feet under his calves. "I get that you're scared," he told her. "No one wants to hurt you. We just want the truth."

To his surprise, she threw back her head and laughed. At least it was something.

"Want to try something more than laughter?" Curtis had joined them on the ground. After a moment, Ohiyesa did so as well.

"I'm not afraid," she said at last, gazing up into the night sky, scrupulously avoiding meeting any of their eyes. "I just know you won't believe anything I say. After all, I'm Madame .44, the Outlaw Queen." She spat this last with contempt.

"Try me." Ohiyesa's voice was quiet, but steady.

Madame .44 sighed heavily, dropping her chin to her chest. "Guess I don't have much of a choice, do I?

"The Clantons in Elkhorn," she began, "are kin to the Clantons back in Mesa City. And *those* Clantons stole a load of silver and a passel of cash from a local church collection to build a new school."

Passel, Cisco mouthed to Curtis excitedly. It was *so* Wild West.

Curtis frowned at him in annoyance. *Listen*, he mouthed back.

"This is a scheme they've been using for years," Madame .44 went on. "The Mesa City branch of the family steals, then ships their spoils up to Elkhorn, where the 'respectable' branch of the family can sell it or trade it for profit. They've been doing it for a long time, but this time I knew about it as soon as it happened, before there was time for the Elkhorn Clantons to resell. So I came after them to take back what they stole."

"Wait." Ohiyesa raised a hand to stop her. "I'm not quite following you. You're Madame .44. You're known across the West as a thief and outlaw. Say I believe you about the Clantons in Mesa—why're you suddenly a Good Samaritan?"

"She's like Robin Hood!" Cisco said enthusiastically. At the dead stares from Ohiyesa and Madame .44, his eyebrows knit together and he wondered aloud: "Wait, have I messed up my history? Has Robin Hood happened yet?"

"Robin Hood was medieval England," Curtis said wearily. "Yes, he's happened. He's just not a common reference point in this country yet."

"You steal from the rich," Cisco explained, "and give to the poor."

Madame .44 shrugged. "Something like that, I suppose. It's easier to get close to outlaws when they think you're one of them."

Ohiyesa rocked back on his heels, sucking in a hot breath. "Whoa. Whoa."

"Did she just blow your mind?" Cisco asked.

Ohiyesa slapped his hands to his head, as though making certain it hadn't gone anywhere. "What? With dynamite? What do you mean?"

"It's a future expression," Curtis told him. "It means . . . did she surprise you?"

"You could say so! Madame .44, scourge of the West, is a saint, not a sinner? I'm gonna need a little more than just her say-so. The Clantons are good people and they say you stole a bunch of heirlooms from them."

Madame .44 shrugged. "One of the silver pieces they stole is an original Paul Revere. Handed down for almost a hundred years. It has his maker's mark on it—you can check. It's a cann with a Revere stamp on the bottom. You'll see."

"Only problem with that," Ohiyesa said after rolling around the idea in his head for a minute, "is that you'd need to show me the stuff you stole. You gotta trust me, Madame .44."

They gazed into each other's eyes for a long, long time, weighing each other, balancing their needs. Then she said, "Fine, Sheriff. I'll show you where I stashed the loot."

Cisco's grin was enormous. "This. Is. So. Cool!" he chortled.

"Geek," Mr. Terrific deadpanned.

Madame .44 claimed to have hidden her "stolen back" property in a cave nearby. The "cave" turned out to be little more than a hole in the side of a low hill.

Cisco offered to go in. Madame .44 was still in handcuffs, Ohiyesa wasn't about to leave her side, and Curtis was a little too big. So Cisco figured he might as well volunteer before he was drafted.

Using the light from his cell phone, he crawled in, then wriggled and shimmied for a few feet. Ahead of him, he spied a worn satchel. It clanked reassuringly when he tugged at it, and soon he was back out in the open air, with a genuine Wild West desperado's satchel in his hands, to boot.

Again: So. Cool.

They dumped out the contents of the bag. Three thick sheaves of paper money that were so hilariously big and colorful that Cisco almost laughed at them. Two silver candlesticks, some jewelry, and then what Madame .44 had called a "cann," which to Cisco's eyes was nothing more than a smallish, widemouthed pitcher cast in silver. He picked it up and turned it over.

The bottom was tarnished, speckled with black patches. He wiped at them, but they remained.

"Sorry," he told Madame .44. "I don't see any mark."

"They knew I was coming for them," she said. "They would have sanded it down."

Ohiyesa sighed. "That's mighty convenient."

Cisco summoned Curtis over. Together, they scrutinized the bottom of the cann. It *did* appear as though some of the blemishes formed a sort of rectangle, just off-center. Cisco ran his thumb over it; it felt slightly recessed.

"Could be," Curtis offered. "But my metallurgical knowledge is really focused on titanium, promethium, stuff like that."

"I have an idea." Cisco took out his phone and snapped a picture of the bottom of the cann. Then he used a photo-editing app to change light levels on the picture. The result was a new image, one that enhanced the subtle depths and gradations of the original.

"You might have to take my word for this . . ." Cisco held out the phone a little hesitantly. "Do you know what a photograph is?"

Ohiyesa peered at the phone. "Sort of like a tintype, no?"

"Close enough."

There, on the phone, the image was grainy but clear, brought into relief by the photo-editing app: a rectangle with the characters REVERE within it.

"Good enough for you, Sheriff?" Curtis asked.

Drawing in a deep breath, Ohiyesa contemplated the phone, then Madame .44. "It's enough for me to rethink all of this. Tell you what, Madame .44—I'll take you back to Elkhorn, and my deputy, Hank Brown, will keep you hidden while I look into this some more. Between you and me and Hank, we'll bring this whole thieving family down. Fair?"

She bit her lip and nodded. "Fair. Thank you, Sheriff." To Cisco and Curtis: "And thank you, too."

"You're welcome." Curtis bowed a bit. Cisco groaned at it.

"All I ask," she said, "is that you not reveal my secret. I'll need to keep pretending to be the 'Outlaw Queen' in order to help people. So please don't tell anyone."

"I won't say a word," Ohiyesa promised.

"Your secret is safe with me," Curtis pledged.

"I'm totally gonna update your Wikipedia page when I get home," Cisco said.

Curtis shoved him. "He'll keep quiet. Don't worry."

"Speaking of getting home . . ." Cisco arched an eyebrow at Curtis. "We need to send a message, don't we?"

"I'll help any way I can," Ohiyesa said. "I appreciate you helping me figure out the truth here. Without you fellas, I'd have done this woman here wrong."

"We want to give you something," Curtis said. "Think of it as a family heirloom. Pass it down. And on a date we're going to give to you, we want you or your descendants to bring it to a specific person at a specific place."

"Sure," said Ohiyesa. "It's the least I can do."

"Music to my ears, Sheriff." Cisco's grin was broad and gleeful. "Music to my ears."

As Ohiyesa and Madame .44 rode off, Curtis turned to Cisco. "Now what do we do?"

"If it works, it should be pretty quick." Cisco lay back on the grass. "So let's just enjoy the stars a little longer, hmm?"

Laughing softly, Curtis joined him.

36

CAITLIN FOUND IRIS STARING INTO a cup of lukewarm coffee in the mess at S.T.A.R. Labs. With rapid strides, she crossed the room and slid into a chair across from Iris. "I have an idea."

Iris didn't look up from her mug. "If it involves microwaving this coffee, I already thought of that. I'm just trying to summon the willpower to move."

"Hey, I get it. Everything's falling apart. As usual. We've been here before. And it's always darkest—"

"Right before you stumble into a pit in the middle of a cave?"

"Well, yeah, technically. But listen, Iris . . ." She reached across the table and put her hand over Iris's. "I have an idea. For real. About getting Cisco back."

At that, Iris raised her gaze. Caitlin Snow seldom exaggerated or overpromised. If she had an idea, then she had an idea. And maybe it would even work.

Getting Cisco back . . . That would be clutch. Felicity was smart when it came to computers and hacking, but Cisco was brilliant *and* a polymath. He could synthesize high explosives out of used gum and aspirin, build a weather control machine out of baling wire and old batteries. His presence would change the complexion of their situation considerably.

"How?" she asked.

Caitlin leaned forward, eager. "Remember when Barry came back from the sixty-fourth century? He told us that everything resonates with vibrations unique to its own place and time in the Multiverse."

"Yeah, I remember. He used some kind of device from the future—"

"The Cosmic Treadmill."

"—Right. He used it to reset his vibrations, and his speed powers let him maintain those vibrations so that he could stay in the sixty-fourth century. Then, when he was done, he just let his vibrations return to normal and he popped back here immediately."

"So . . ." Caitlin's eyes danced with excitement. "So, what if we had a way to lock in on Cisco's vibrations? And then reset them? He'd pop back here instantly."

Iris frowned. "How would we do that?"

Digging into her lab coat's big pocket, Caitlin produced a familiar set of sunglasses. Cisco's "Vibe" shades. The ones he wore when he was out super-heroing. He'd taken them from the evil Earth 2 version of Cisco Ramon, then modified them for his own use. The sunglasses helped Cisco control and exploit his powers to their utmost.

"He left these behind when he went to help the others close the breach. The sunglasses are already attuned to Cisco's unique vibrational pattern because he uses them to *adjust* those vibrations when he uses his powers." Caitlin's words tumbled out in a rush. "We can use these to give us a baseline, then use Reverse-Flash's time sphere in the Starchives to go fishing in the time stream."

Iris plucked the goggles from Caitlin's fingers and stared at them. "And reel in our Cisco."

For the first time in days, she allowed her lips to relax into a grin. "This just might work, Caitlin!" Triumphantly, she raised her coffee mug and took a big gulp . . .

Which she promptly spat out. "Right. Probably should have microwaved that after all. C'mon, let's go tell Felicity your idea and see if she can help us make it work."

Felicity listened as Caitlin and Iris described exactly what they needed from her. Then she blew a stray lock of blonde hair out of her eyes and ticked items off on her fingers as she spoke:

"So . . . you guys want me to take Earth 2 tech from these goggles and route it through a twenty-fourth-century time machine's circuitry in order to 'go fishing' in the river of time, looking for Cisco? Really?"

"Really." Iris bobbed her head eagerly. "Can you do it?"

Felicity thought about it. "But what if Cisco and Curtis

aren't together? Or what if it only yanks Cisco back and leaves Curtis wherever he is, alone?"

"Then at least we'll have Cisco back," Caitlin said, "and he can help us retrieve Curtis."

"Look, Felicity," Iris said, "this isn't just our best chance to get things moving. It's our *only* chance. You're great, but—"

"But you need your genial mad scientist back. I get it."

"No offense," Caitlin said hurriedly.

"None taken." Felicity tugged her hair into a ponytail. "If I'm gonna do this, I'm going to have to . . ."

She broke off at a bleating sound from a nearby control panel and shot out of her chair.

"That's not an alarm!" Iris assured her. "It's the doorbell."

"Your doorbell just gave me a heart attack!"

Iris fiddled with a knob, and the big screen showed the main outer door into S.T.A.R. Labs. A tall, handsome Native American man stood there. He wore khaki pants, a white dress shirt with no tie, a blue windbreaker, and an expression of barely controlled frustration. It was the sort of look a man acquired after standing in a steady drizzle for an annoying and unnecessary half hour.

"Oh, that's the guy," Caitlin said. "The one I told you about before. Smith. The one who's been wanting to talk to you."

"Persistent, isn't he? I can't believe he's back." Iris studied him. He clearly wanted to ring the bell again but managed to restrain himself. "OK, fine. I'll talk to him. Felicity, can you get started on the time retrieval whatever-it-is?"

Felicity threw her hands up in the air. "I don't even know

where to start! But, sure! Why not? It's just elaborate quantum physics and intricate nano-engineering to wrangle the fundamental forces of the universe."

Iris pretended not to pick up on the sarcasm in Felicity's voice as she breezed past her on her way out of the Cortex. "Great! You and Caitlin get to work—I'll go see what Agent Smith needs and get him off our backs."

Smith was waiting for her in the S.T.A.R. Labs lobby, gazing at a pedestal that had a plaque embedded in it. Iris knew the words by heart:

YOU ARE STANDING ON THE VERY SPOT WHERE HARRISON ROBERT WELLS FIRST IMBIBED MOROCCAN BLEND. Along with a date and time.

"This is helpful information," he said to her without preamble as she entered.

Iris extended a hand to him. "We had a friend with plans to turn this place into a museum. He was fiddling around with different ideas. Pleased to meet you, Agent Smith. I'm Iris West-Allen. I don't mean to be brusque, but we're swamped. What can I do for you?"

Smith took her hand and shook. "Not agent. Marshal. U.S. Marshal Ohiyesa Smith."

"Oh. I'm sorry. I didn't realize you were a marshal. Look, you should still be liaising directly with CCPD. Captain David Singh is—"

He broke in, clearly not interested. "Mrs. West-Allen, I'm not here as part of a task force or any sort of relief organization.

You guys had a big blowup downtown? Great. I don't care. That's not why I'm here."

Taken aback, Iris blinked. Smith was intense. Like, Oliver Queen intense. "Marshal Smith, I've got four or five crises going on at the same time. If you're not here to help, can you plan to be a pain in my butt some other day?"

He chuckled without mirth and scrounged for something in the pocket of his windbreaker. He spoke as though he hadn't heard a single word she'd said. "When I was a kid, my great-grandfather died. Boo-hoo, everyone was sad. Whatever. I hardly knew him. I was named for him, though, and I guess that connected us in some way."

"That's sad and heartwarming, Marshal, but—"

He cut her off with a glance, finally producing a small beaded bag from his pocket. "My grandfather died about ten years ago. And my dad is sick, so it fell to me. I was supposed to be here a couple of days ago, but air traffic in and out of the area was restricted after the . . . whatever it was that happened here." He held out the bag to her.

"What's this?"

"Look inside."

She peered into the bag. There was a smallish package in there, wrapped in what looked like leather.

"If there's one thing my people know, it's how to preserve things," Smith told her. "My grandfather used to wrap his hunting rifle in deerskin and leave it in the top of the trees when hunting season was out. He'd come back months later and it was fine. Would have lasted a hundred years, easy."

Iris pulled out the hide-wrapped package and started unwrapping it.

"More than a hundred years ago, my great-grandfather met a man named Cisco Ramon."

Iris's jaw dropped at Cisco's name. She couldn't move. Smith's piercing black eyes held hers for an extended moment.

"Keep unwrapping. The story in my family is that Cisco was from the future. I always thought that sounded a little hinky, but we live in a strange world, so who knows? Anyway, Cisco gave old Ohiyesa what's in this bag and asked him to hand it down through his family, until this date, at which point it was to be delivered to this place. To you."

Iris finished unwrapping the package. It was a cell phone. And just as Smith had promised, just like his grandfather's hunting rifle, it was in terrific condition.

"I . . . Thank you, Marshal. I'm sorry I made you wait. I didn't know."

Ohiyesa Smith clucked his tongue. "I'm just glad to cross this off my list. I've been hearing about this since I was a kid. Always knew there was a chance I'd be the one to deliver it. I can't say I cotton much to being an errand boy, but I'm told it's for a good cause."

"It is," Iris said, staring down at the phone. It was Cisco's, all right. She recognized the tattered remains of the *Star Wars* sticker he'd affixed to the back. He had applied it new three days ago, and now it was more than a century old. Tears welled up in her eyes. "Thank you so much."

37

THE SKIES OVER SMALLVILLE slowly began clearing as the day wore on. Barry and Oliver worked with Alex's team of DEO agents to return the evacuees. One kid—maybe twelve, maybe thirteen—turned to Barry after the Flash had deposited him safely at home, and said, "I haven't seen *anything* about you on the Internet. You're so cool!"

Barry grinned at him and gave him a thumbs-up. "Thanks."

"Can you teach me how to run fast?" the kid asked eagerly. "I'm super-slow and I'm always late to everything."

It helps if you get hit by lightning and doused in chemicals, Barry thought but didn't say. The last thing he needed was the youth of Earth 38 going around with car batteries and chemistry sets, trying to replicate his powers.

"Believe it or not," he told the kid, "I'm always late, too. It's not about when you arrive—it's about what you do once you're there."

• • •

Later, they all gathered at the Kent Farm. *All* meaning Oliver, Barry, Brainy, Lena, Alex, and J'Onn. Superman was still at his Fortress, having messaged back a few hours earlier that Kara was in stable condition and would recover.

"History records that Supergirl died on this day," Brainy said with mingled shock and disbelief in his voice.

"History was wrong," Oliver said.

"It's not the first time," Barry said, thinking of Flashpoint. He had never felt more relief and gratitude in his life.

There were still remnants of Anti-Matter Man adrift in the air and scattered around Smallville, each one composed of potent anti-matter that could cause deadly explosions and toxic leak-

age. Lena and Brainy developed a special energy cage to contain those fragments, and there was a team of DEO agents scouring the ground and sky to collect them all. Eventually, the red sky over Smallville would dissipate and the days would be clear once more. J'Onn had already flown Lena and Brainy's breach-closing device into the sky and shut down the breach to Earth 27. They were safe. The threat from the antiverse was defeated.

And for now . . . they needed a break.

J'Onn proved surprisingly adept at the farm's old-fashioned stove, turning out a series of omelets and hash browns for the starving crew. Barry reminded himself to eat slowly, lest he polish off everything in sight before anyone else could get a forkful in their mouth.

"Best eggs I've ever had," Oliver admitted.

"The Kents were known for their poultry products," Alex

told them. "Something about county fairs and blue ribbons. I never paid much attention. But . . ." She fixed Barry with a glare and went on:

"But when I ask you for a sitrep, I expect to get one, buster."

"That became dark very quickly," Lena observed.

"Sorry, Alex. I was trying to protect you."

"Good thing Superman got there when he did," Oliver commented. "It was touch and go."

"Thank you for your sensitive appraisal of the situation," Alex said sarcastically.

With a shrug, Oliver said, "I call them as I see them."

"If I may interrupt with a . . . pragmatic matter," Brainy said. "While we may have eliminated the threat of Anti-Matter Man, there is still the issue of how he was released. And why."

Barry nodded, a thoughtful expression on his face. "He attacked here, but thanks to J'Onn we know now that he was being controlled by someone in the future."

"The *far* future," Oliver put in.

"The really, *really* far future," Lena said, chewing through her eggs. "It's mind-boggling in a way I have trouble even imagining."

Barry had been to the sixty-fourth century, but even that seemed like a mere tomorrow compared to the end of Time itself.

"The best defense is a good offense," said Oliver. "If someone at the end of Time is our enemy, then it's time for us to stop waiting for him to attack . . ."

". . . and make a move of our own," Alex agreed. "But how?"

Barry grinned. "I think I know some people who can help us . . ."

"I like your confidence," said Oliver, "but do you care to let the rest of us in on the secret?"

"One moment." Brainy suddenly stood, ramrod stiff. "I'm receiving a massive data download from the DEO. A security protocol I enacted when we first became aware of Anti-Matter Man."

"What is it?" Alex demanded.

Brainy's eyes fluttered for an instant, processing. "Enormous fluctuations in the quantum foam . . ." He grimaced and looked around the room, taking in their surprised expressions, painted with dread.

"It's not over yet," he told them.

38

CISCO WAS ALIVE. OR HAD BEEN, AT least, more than a hundred years ago. A small part of Iris—a part she suppressed and smothered into silence with the busyness of each day—had known that there was always a chance that Cisco and Curtis had died in the explosion. Or been killed when they emerged from the time stream. But now she knew. They'd survived.

And now they had a date. A rough location.

More than that: They had a way to get Curtis and Cisco back.

"Felicity!" she shouted, striding into the Cortex. "Stop what you're doing! We have another way!"

"Well, that's good," Caitlin said. "Because all we've done so far is read half the Wikipedia entry on time travel."

"They make it sound so easy," Felicity grumbled. "*They're* not the ones with two people stuck in an unknowable past."

"Not unknowable anymore." Iris gently placed the phone on the console before them. "The battery probably died around 1900, but can you get this running again? We've got a time machine to build."

Felicity's eyes widened. "Is this a cell phone from the Wild West?"

"This is in fact a cell phone from the Wild West," Iris said with satisfaction.

With a squeal of glee, Felicity snatched it up and ran to a workstation.

Cisco's phone hadn't survived 150 years entirely intact. Ohiyesa Smith and his family had taken good care of it, but that was still a long time to wait.

Felicity was able to disassemble it and pry out the necessary chips, which she then transferred to a new phone. Soon, they were playing a video. Cisco's face loomed large on the screen.

"Hello, people of the twenty-first century!" he said, and Iris almost broke down at the sound of his voice. Caitlin grabbed her hand and squeezed.

Curtis poked his head in from the side. "Hello, everyone! The Wild West is fine. Wish you were here."

"No, no," Cisco said. "Wish *we* were *there*. So let's get started."

They watched the video twice, just to be sure. Cisco told them exactly where in his workshop the time-retrieval gear was stowed. He also said—three separate times, "This is a prototype. Be very careful with it! I'm not there to fix it if you break it!"

They recovered Danger Box 3C from the Dark Lab. It was smaller than you'd think for something containing so complicated a device. Composed of a light but strong alloy Cisco had stumbled upon while trying to figure out the best way to shield himself from the use of his own cold gun, it measured no more than a foot on each side. A deep gray in color, it iridesced in the light of the Cortex. A ten-digit mantissa keypad was mounted on the front.

Cisco had given them the passcode to the box in his video, and when Iris punched it in, the box's lid opened without complaint. Within, they spied a handheld gadget that looked like a cross between a set of brass knuckles and a video game controller; it had red lights running around it. Connected to that by a set of thin cables was a mesh dome with more lights.

"So . . ." Felicity lifted the equipment out of the box *very* carefully, lest she rip out one of those fragile cables. "According to Cisco, now what?"

Caitlin skimmed the notes she'd taken during their re-watch of the video. "We need a 'vibrational pattern match source.'" Her lips twisted in confusion for a moment, but then her eyes lit up. "The goggles! See? I knew it!"

She hauled the goggles out of her lab coat pocket and handed them over to Iris, who waggled them at Felicity.

Who shrugged.

"Yeah, OK, it can't be any harder than soldering a motherboard, right? Give me some time with this stuff and we'll see about getting the boys back."

In less time than Iris feared, Felicity managed to connect

Cisco's Vibe goggles to the time-retrieval device. The welds were sloppy and ugly, but they held.

"So, it looks like you put the dome on your head . . ." Felicity said, miming donning a hat, "then slip this controller thing on your hand . . . And fire at will."

All three looked at one another.

"Hey," Felicity said, breaking the silence. "I put it together. I'm not wearing it and ending up in medieval Scotland or something. My hair needs *way* too much product to maintain this bounce and shine. No one's *Outlander*ing me."

"Your confidence in your handiwork is palpable," Iris deadpanned.

"Not *my* handiwork. That sucker is hardwired in there. But Cisco's record isn't exactly spotless, you know."

Caitlin nudged Iris out of the way and picked up the device. "For God's sake. I'll do it."

"Are you sure?" By the time the words were out of Iris's mouth, Caitlin had already slipped the dome over her head and tugged the controller over the fingers of her right hand. With the wires connecting them and the goggles fused to the back of the "helmet" thanks to Felicity's soldering, Caitlin looked like the world's worst and lowest-tech cyborg.

"Do I just press this— Whoa!"

Caitlin had thumbed a big red button on the controller as she asked. An immediate surge of energy lit up all the red lights on the hand device, then raced up the wires to illuminate a series of red, yellow, and blue lights on the mesh dome perched atop her head. At the same time, a high-pitched whine sounded in the room.

"Don't point it at me!" Felicity yelled. Caitlin had been holding out her hand in Felicity's direction when she started her question.

Whipping around, Caitlin pointed her fist at the far side of the Cortex. The whine built, rising in frequency such that Iris's molars started to vibrate. She could only imagine what it was like for Caitlin, at the very center of it. A coruscating halo of energy encircled her friend, who now brought up her left hand to grab her own right wrist, steadying that arm as it jittered and shook with the influx of power.

"Get . . . back . . . !" Caitlin managed to yell.

"Oh, hell no!" Felicity shouted. At the same moment, she and Iris dived toward Caitlin. Felicity grabbed her around the waist to steady her; Iris reached around to help stabilize her arm.

"Too . . . much . . . !" Caitlin howled. The air in the room, displaced by the ferocious heat and energy from the time-retrieval device, began to shift and whip and scream. It was like shoving a tornado into a box. "Get . . . out of . . . here!"

"Not a chance!" Iris yelled to her. "We're not leaving you!"

Caitlin bellowed in pain, and her entire body stiffened as a bolt of lightning erupted from her right hand and lashed out into the Cortex. Before it could hit anything, though, it exploded on its own, as if it had crashed against some invisible barrier.

Much to Iris's shock, she witnessed a breach forming where the lightning bolt had scattered. Unlike the bluish breaches she was used to—and unlike the reddish one that had portended Anti-Matter Man's arrival—this one was a hard yellow, like the visual remnant of the sun against the back of your eyelids when you close your eyes. It crackled and throbbed like a wound.

"I think it's working!" She had to scream to be heard over the whine of Cisco's gadget, the sizzle and hiss of the breach, her own thudding heartbeat in her ears.

"How can you tell?" Felicity cried out.

Turning, she saw that Felicity's hair was standing on end, a golden peacock's fan dancing to its own tune. Her own hair was doing the same, she realized. Only Caitlin's remained flat, held down by the mesh dome atop her head.

How can I tell? I don't know how to answer that. You've never time-traveled—I've been there when Barry's done it. And this just feels right.

"How long should this take anyway?" Curtis asked Cisco.

"How am I supposed to know?"

"You're the time travel guy."

Cisco grunted noncommittally. "I don't know. Relativistically, it should have happened by now, but one thing I've learned about time travel is that you're basically never on time. You always— Yikes!"

As he'd spoken, the air around them suddenly went electric. Sparks jumped and spat. The two of them leaped up from their relaxed poses on the ground. A whirl of yellow light spun into existence before them, crackling with power.

"Is this it?" Curtis yelled above the noise of the breach.

"If it isn't, it's a heck of a coincidence!" Cisco replied.

Two shadows appeared at the center of the breach, their edges fuzzy and indistinct.

"It's them!" Iris yelled. "Hold on, Caitlin!"

"I'm trying!" Sweat poured down Caitlin's face, clinging to her eyelashes and flicking into the air with each exhale of breath. "I'm trying!"

Cisco held up his hand to shield his eyes from the tremendous light of the breach. He'd never seen one like this before. Granted, it was generated by imperfect equipment, but for a doorway home, it still looked pretty dangerous.

"Are we supposed to go *into* that?" Curtis sounded incredulous. "It feels like it would fry us before it would take us home."

"Only one way to find out!" And with that, Cisco took a cautious step toward the present.

One of the figures tried to take a step forward, but some force prevented it. The figure jerked back.

Felicity risked letting go of Caitlin. "Can you hold her steady?" she barked to Iris. "I want to try something!"

Iris bobbled her head, her hair wildly spinning as she did so. With a murmured apology that she was sure went unheard, she clutched Caitlin tighter, hugging her friend to her body as though trying to save her from drowning. It was like snuggling up to a space heater—a hum, heat, light, power, pain.

Felicity broke away and scrambled to one of the desks, shoving the wheeled chair out of the way. It rolled ten feet away, slipping between Caitlin and the breach. A spark of electricity hit it and sent it flying across the room, where it collided with the wall and lay there, charred and smoldering.

Cisco stumbled backward, colliding fully with Curtis, who almost fell down. Clutching and clawing at each other for a vertiginous moment, they somehow managed to remain standing. The breach still howled and sizzled before them.

"They need more vibrational energy," Cisco realized. "They

don't have enough to bring us through."

"And we have no way to tell them," Curtis said.

Gritting her teeth to focus through the distractions around her, Felicity called up the control system for the Cortex's public address system. All around her, the air grew hotter and more charged with electricity. It would have to be soon, or they would die before they could get Cisco and Curtis through.

There was no time to plan or prepare. Felicity cranked up the volume on the Cortex's speakers, then slid the controls on the equalizer all the way up, setting the bass to its highest level. She needed vibrations. It was all about vibrations.

"Felicity!" Iris. In a rare panic. "Whatever you're going to do, do it *now*!"

Felicity took note of the song queued up on her phone:

"Extreme Ways" by Moby. An oldie, but a goodie. Oliver ran to it on the treadmill sometimes.

She hit play, and the first string line sang out, blasted over the powerful speakers. It shook her jaw and sent a line of pain from one ear to the other, spiking her brain on the way. Then the bass line kicked in—and the room thrummed like the front row at a rock concert.

"*This* is your plan?" Iris screamed, shooting a death glare back over her shoulder at Felicity. "A *soundtrack?*"

Before Felicity could explain, Caitlin called out, barely audible over all the noise: "I think it's working!"

"Then it fell apart!" Moby sang at a truly obscene decibel level.

Caitlin ground her teeth together. She tasted blood in her mouth. A tooth was coming loose. That one she'd cracked as a kid, biting into some too-hard Halloween candy. She'd had it capped, and now the cap was disconnecting from the enamel. Ten years with no dental work down the drain. Oh well. If she had to lose a few teeth to save the world, that was a small price to pay.

Something changed in the breach. The center of it was becoming clearer. The muzzy shadow figures crisped and became more distinct at the edges. One of them was tall, lanky. The other shorter, with an outline of ponytail.

Curtis. Cisco. It was working.

The sound coming from the breach jumped in volume and in pitch, even as the spinning, whirling yellow edges intensified, setting the night ablaze as though with another sun.

Curtis hung back. "What do we do? It looks too powerful!"

245

"I don't know!" Cisco cast about, looking for anything at all that could help, that could provide an answer. But there was nothing. No one.

Just him.

He focused and thrust out his hands, zapping a vibe blast at the breach. There was a sound like glass scraping against glass, and Cisco screamed.

If anything, the breach looked even more dangerous.

"We go through now!" Cisco yelled.

"Are you sure?" Curtis looked from him to the breach and back again doubtfully. "It doesn't seem—"

"On the other side of that breach is a caffè macchiato and Netflix!" Cisco told him. "Go!"

"We needed more vibrational energy!" Felicity yelled as she rejoined Caitlin and Iris. But it was pointless to talk—no one could hear her over the music, the wind, the machinery, the hiss and spit of electricity, and the low thrum of the breach. She could scarcely hear her own voice.

So she focused on helping to steady Caitlin, who was beginning to slide ever so slowly across the floor toward the breach. They wanted things to come *out*, not to go *in*.

As they watched, the breach flickered, its yellow light going green, then red, then blue, then a bright white for just an instant. A second later, the two figures stumbled through the breach.

"Shut it down!" Iris screamed, but no one could hear. Caitlin's eyes were screwed tightly shut, and she didn't even know Cisco and Curtis had come through.

So Iris reached over, grabbed the cables connecting the helmet to the hand control, and yanked. It was only in the instant that she felt the cables come loose that it occurred to her that this might be an exceptionally bad idea. That maybe simply pulling the plug would make things worse.

Just then, the whine from the machinery went away. At the same moment, in an amazing coincidence, the music stopped playing. The breach settled into a reliable sort of blue pulse, steadily beginning to shrink. The silence was so big and so all-consuming that Iris thought she might go deaf from the pounding of her own heartbeat.

Curtis and Cisco had collided with each other on reentry and crashed to the floor. Now Mr. Terrific rose to his feet, leaning down to help Cisco up.

"I told you it would work!" Cisco chortled. "Cisco Ramon always—"

With a sound like a thousand shattering windows, an enormous hand reached through the shrinking breach. It wore what looked like a gunmetal glove, form-fitting. The gigantic fingers closed around Cisco, who yelped once as he was dragged toward the breach.

"*I have need of you, Cisco Ramon,*" said a voice like oil and gravel.

And then Cisco disappeared into the breach, and the breach itself pinched shut, vanishing like a thin-skinned soap bubble on a hot summer's day.

"What . . . What just happened?" Curtis spun around, gazing in every direction. "What just *happened*?"

Caitlin wiped a film of blood from her lips. "Where did he go?" She knocked her palm against her right ear. "Can anyone hear me? Can you hear me?" Shouting into the quiet.

"We can hear you, Caitlin." Iris took her friend's hands, gripped them hard, fixed her eyes with her own. She spoke with exaggerated mouth movements, to make it easier for Caitlin to read her lips. "You did it, OK? You're just a little deaf. We all are right now."

Caitlin seemed to get it, nodded, but pulled away from Iris. "Where's Cisco?" she said loudly. "I saw him. Where'd he go?"

"Something came through," said Felicity. "Something took him."

They peered around the room, as though expecting the hand to come back any moment, even though the breach was gone.

The ceiling began to flash red. An alarm sounded. The big monitor screen lit up with the image of Joe West, panic in his eyes.

"We have a serious problem here in Star City! Ambush Bug's planning to unleash a swarm! We don't know what that means, but at the very least, a bunch of people who don't know they're allergic to bees are gonna die! We have no way to stop him! Get Barry back from Earth 38 *now!*"

"Dad," Iris began, "we can't just yank him back here . . ."

The alarm was still going off; the red lights kept flashing. Curtis collapsed into a chair, exhausted, depleted, his face twisted into utter shock and despair.

Leaning on Felicity, Caitlin made her way to another chair and dropped into it. "Wait!" she yelled, still trying to be heard over her own deafness. "That's the TroubleAlert! For multiverse incursions!"

Felicity glanced at the screen. "She's right! Oh my God! According to this, there are spikes of quantum foam . . ." She ran her hands over the controls, scanning the data. "Breaches are opening everywhere! We have people coming out from all over the multiverse . . . and people falling *in* . . ."

"Hold on!" Iris ordered. One crisis at a time. "Felicity, track those breaches. Dad, we have our own—"

"Oh no!" Curtis warned and struggled to rise from his seat.

"Iris?" Joe asked. "Iris, baby, what's happening there? What are you all looking at?" The camera angle kept Joe from seeing what they saw as they all turned to the Cortex entrance. There stood Madame Xanadu.

Stood was probably the wrong word. Groggy and still not fully healed, she leaned against a tall, broad-shouldered man who wore a loose-fitting gray boilersuit with blue boots, blue trunks, a yellow belt, and a blue cloak. His face was framed by an open cowl that resembled an owl's head.

He held a knife to Madame Xanadu's throat.

Even with his hair and ears covered, he looked familiar to Iris . . .

"My name is Bruce Wayne," the man said, his lips twisting into something between a smile and a sneer. "But you'll probably feel more comfortable calling me Owlman. Don't worry—I'm here to save the world."

EPILOGUE

MICK RORY CRAWLED.

He'd been crawling a long time. The muscles in his legs had seized up awhile ago, gone useless from lack of water. It was too hot here. Even at night, which was short. Too many suns for there to be a long night. Three moons at night and at least three suns during the day. He'd stopped counting them because his vision was blurring and he couldn't be sure he was seeing straight any longer.

It had rained from the black clouds, but it hadn't been water. Not exactly. It had sizzled when it hit the ground around him, and it felt slick and oily on his skin. As thirsty as he was, he couldn't bear to let it pass his lips, and when the rain stopped, he was grateful.

But he'd watched those suns set and the thirst hit hard, and he'd wished he'd changed his mind before the not-water all evaporated away. Death by poison would be preferable to death by thirst, he thought.

The pain was absolute and all-encompassing. He crawled because he had to move, because to drag himself along this desert toward *somewhere*, anywhere, was better than just lying in the wreckage of the *Waverider* and waiting for death.

He wondered: Would Len be waiting for him when he died?

Probably not. Len—Captain Cold, Mick's old partner in crime—had sacrificed himself. Joined the Legends, like Mick, but unlike Mick, he managed to accrue a little nobility along the way. Gave up his life for the universe. That kind of thing. Went out a hero.

Len would get the choirs of angels and the harps and the all-you-can-eat heavenly buffet. Mick knew he'd made up for a lot of the bad he'd done in his own life, but he'd never truly repented. He figured he was headed the other way.

That's OK. He liked fire.

Using his elbows, he pulled himself along some more. There was a ridge in the distance, and he'd convinced himself that if he could get there, everything would be OK. It was a foolish thing to believe, but what else did he have going for him? There was no one else to lie to and no one else to lie for him. He had to do it himself.

A sound came to him. There was wind here, and occasionally it made a whistling noise. But this was different.

He looked up.

Above him, a shadow moved. It hovered into place. Then, very gently, it grew larger and larger.

Something was moving. Not one of those strange black clouds—something else entirely.

As he watched, the shadow took on a defined shape—a long, cigar-shaped body with a disk at one end. A ship. A spaceship.

It landed not far from him. Mick's instincts told him to run, but his legs told him *not a chance.*

So he could do nothing but watch, helpless, as a hatch opened. A figure stood there and then . . .

And then the figure *flew* to him.

Mick had seen a lot as a Legend. A lot of history. A lot of the future. For some reason, watching people *fly* unassisted shocked him every single time. It was freeing and astonishing and so, so deeply unnatural.

The figure landed near him. Mick caught a glimpse of yellow boots that led to a skintight red bodysuit with flaring shoulders. Red gloves and yellow sleeves. Yellow trunks. A sun emblem on the chest.

It was a kid. A redheaded kid, no older than eighteen or nineteen. Just flying around the universe in a spaceship.

Sure. Sure, *that* made sense.

"🝰🝱🝲 🝳🝴🝵 🝶🝷🝸?" the kid asked.

And Mick laughed. For all he knew, the kid was wondering if Mick tasted good with ketchup and mustard.

"No hablo español," Mick growled. "Come back when you talk American."

The kid blinked, then smiled. "Oh," he said. "You speak ancient English! So do I!"

He crouched down next to Mick and made a fist, then spoke in his weird language directly into a ring he wore on that hand.

Something came back that sounded professional by the tone of it.

"Everything is all right," the kid said, smiling even more broadly. "I'm Sun Boy. You've been rescued by the Legion of Super-Heroes."

TO BE CONTINUED . . .

It's time for the Crisis to end!

Ambush Bug is about to make everyone in Star City either dead or insane. Plus, the Flash and his allies are prepared to do the impossible and travel to the end of Time in order to face their mystery foe. How does Owlman fit in? What has happened to Cisco?

Not one, but two realities are in jeopardy, and only the Flash is fast enough to save the day. But is there any chance for Barry Allen to come out of this alive?

ACKNOWLEDGMENTS

My heartfelt thanks to those who conjured Supergirl and kept her going all these years, especially folks like Otto Binder, Jim Mooney, Paul Kupperberg, Carmine Infantino, Sterling Gates, and Jamal Igle. And I am so very, very grateful to Cynthia Leitich Smith and Joseph Bruchac for their kindness and generosity in discussing Native American history, culture, and traditions with me. They made Ohiyesa such a joy to write, and I thank them for their time.

I am grateful to the folks at Warner Bros. and the CW who make these books possible, especially Carl Ogawa, Victoria Selover, and Josh Anderson, but also to Greg Berlanti, Todd Helbing, Sarah Schechter, Lindsay Kiesel, Janice Aquilar-Herrero, Catherine Shin, Thomas Zellers, and Kristin Chin.

And my undying thanks to my partner in crime and editor, Russ Busse, along with the rest of the hardworking crew at Abrams—including but not limited to Andrew Smith, Jody Mosley, Maggie Lehrman, Marie Oishi, John Passineau, Alison Gervais, Melanie Chang, Maya Bradford, Kim Lauber, Trish McNamara O'Neil, Brooke Shearhouse, and Borana Greku.

And as we wind toward the End of Time, my eternal gratitude to my wife and children, who are my everyday superheroes.

ABOUT THE AUTHOR

BARRY LYGA is the author of the *New York Times* bestselling I Hunt Killers series and many other critically acclaimed middle-grade and young adult novels. A self-proclaimed Flash fanatic, Barry lives and podcasts near New York City with his family. Find him online at barrylyga.com.